R.2

@LIV

Red Hide

The trouble really started when the likeable Billy Dale was murdered shortly after leaving the Bayner ranch, where he had been courting young Rosa. But the mystery was why such a harmless man had been killed and, worse still, scalped.

Jed Bayner was determined to solve the mystery and find the killers. He soon found himself up against the powerful Downey Hollister, a one-armed maniac fired with the aim of killing every Indian in sight. Jed quickly discovered Hollister was going to string him up too. . . .

It would all culminate in a bloody showdown with few standing and the outcome always in doubt. Could justice prevail?

Red Hide

LOUIS CHEVRON

A Black Horse Western

ROBERT HALE · LONDON

Typeset by
Derek Doyle & Associates, Liverpool.
Printed and bound in Great Britain by
Antony Rowe Limited, Wiltshire.

ONE
Loco Rider

Mrs Kate Bayner listened fearfully to the man screaming vilely in Kiowa, then she tried the window shutter bolts once more in the sod-roofed ranchhouse. She shivered, as if she was out there in the cool night air that swept over this part of the Kansas valley, but the shiver was because of the gnawing fright that had assailed her when she first heard the voice. So he had returned. A year had passed since the last time and she had thought – and hoped – that he had died, possibly of an illness or the malnutrition that could hit an old, mad drifter who cared little for his own well-being.

The madman's voice was now only a faint howl on the night wind. Maybe he was riding away – for good, she hoped. And maybe he'd die. He could fall off his horse and break his neck. On the other hand, he'd probably ride off to his hideout in the hills and stay there for another year, getting so crazy that few would take any notice of his babbling. Already most people figured he was a typical loco rider, a strange man made mad by the lonely hills and his solitary existence.

Rosa walked in from the big stone-floored kitchen where she had been helping with the cooking, making scones and bread for the return of her brothers, Jed and Mick. They would be back tomorrow, hungry and glad to be home after the long ride from Wichita.

Her dark eyes flashing inquiringly, Rosa asked, 'What was that strange crying out in the night?'

Kate Bayner turned away. 'Oh, you mean that noise? I guess it was the wind screaming.'

'It sounded like a man's voice . . . shouting . . .'

'Nonsense, girl. The wind plays tricks on the ears – you know that.'

'But I heard Kiowa,' persisted the girl. 'Could it be an Indian out there?'

Kate Bayner said sharply, 'Of course not! Why would an Indian be riding the night trail? I tell you it was the wind. Kiowa, indeed! Really, Rosa, you're letting your imagination run riot.'

The girl went to the big fireplace and stirred the embers with a long iron poker. 'I wish Jed was here. He'd know if it was the wind.'

'He'll be back – and Mick – with all the stores we need. Tomorrow will be a fine day and you'll forget this awful night wind.'

Rosa smiled. She was so unlike her mother. She was dark-haired, and her long tresses were coiled in a bun at the back of her neck though there were times when she let her hair hang free, when she rode the wide range and felt a strange affinity with the distant hills, the purple sage and the hot sun. Her figure in her long calico dress was slim and supple but womanly.

Kate Bayner was almost fifty and grey-haired. A widow for many years, with Jed and Mick helping her on the cattle ranch, and doing a man's work even before they were grown up, she showed all the signs of a hard life. She was plump, with a round face and grey eyes. Her hands were roughened by continuous housework and from earlier years when she had helped with a branding-iron. She would never let Rosa work too hard. Neither would Jed nor Mick, for Rosa was the baby of the family.

Rosa went back to the kitchen, leaving her mother to stare blindly at the shutter covering the window.

He had probably ridden away, she thought, for the crazy screaming in English and Kiowa had stopped. She gripped the back of a chair with knuckles that showed white and muttered, 'Curse you, Simon Greer! Why don't you die?'

Rosa Bayner was down by the creek the next morning. The ranchhouse was almost a mile away, and her ground-hitched pony was nibbling at grass. Suddenly she looked up, startled, and she saw a tall, thin rider. His horse stood on a grassy knoll. He sat motionless, watching her, his face in shadow. But she could see that he was an oldish man and his hat and coat were ragged. There was something odd about his eyes. With a sharp jerk of realization, she knew one eye was screwed up. There was no eyeball. The flesh was wrinkled around a horrible hole.

As she stared, a little afraid, the man slowly pointed an arm at her, accusing, menacing. He emitted a high-pitched, shrill scream that clawed through the air and then tailed off into a few intelligible words.

'Curse you, bitch! A-yaka a-gumba.'

The last words were Kiowa talk. But she couldn't understand for she didn't know enough Kiowa. But in a flash she knew this man had been outside the house last night. It was he who'd made the unearthly sounds.

'Who are you?' she asked suddenly angry.

'You are cursed!' the reedy voice shrilled, then the man put heels to his horse and rode off.

Red Hide

Rosa jumped to her pony, mounted and rode for the ranchhouse. Her mother had lied last night. Surely she had known that the wind had not made the unholy yells and screams.

Before Rosa got very far she looked back. The lone rider was shaking a fist at the morning sky and singing wildly. Rosa ran her pony into the corral at the side of the house. She rushed into the big living room and her mother turned from her sewing, her keen eyes reading what was written in the girl's face.

'Ma, who is that man?'

'What man, child?'

'The crazy man – the one who was screaming at us last night. I just saw him down by the creek. What does he want?'

'I don't know of any man.' Kate Bayner avoided the girl's gaze. 'What are you talking about?'

'He said I was cursed.'

'Who?'

'The strange man. He had one eye. He shouted at me in Kiowa. Why Ma? Why should he shout in Kiowa?'

'You must be mistaken. Rosa, can't you find some work to do? You could help me with that tub of washing.'

'I offered to help an hour ago. Ma, that man frightened me.'

9

Kate Bayner smiled. '*You* – afraid? I've never seen you afraid of anything – even when the Kiowa war party rode up that day. You . . .' She broke off and bit her lip. 'Now, let's have no more of this foolish talk. Help me with that tub, girl.'

Rosa's perplexed feelings lasted for only half an hour. Then they had a caller, a young man she had known all her life. At nineteen, he was a year older than Rosa.

'Why, hello, Billy. Did you ride fourteen miles just to see me? My, but you look good in that suit.'

Billy Dale slid down from his big chestnut mare, adjusted his derby hat and dusted down his thick tweed suit. 'It's new, Rosa. I put it on specially 'cause I figured to see you.' He remembered his manners and whipped off his hat, his moon-like face creasing in a wide grin. 'I said I'd come a'courtin', Rosa.'

'So you did – at the dance – two weeks ago.'

'My pa has kept me busy on the farm. What with milkin' cows and ploughin', he don't give me much time off.'

'Which serves you right, you poor old homesteader. You should stick to longhorns and free range . . .'

'Pa says we've got to farm. He says that's where the future of the country lies.'

She laughed at his round face and carroty hair

10

and the obvious fact that he was scared stiff of her. She thought fleetingly of her elder brother Jed and his confident manner with all the girls at the dance in Winton. Strangely, she had felt a terrible sense of jealousy. Billy Dale had seemed such a clumsy idiot. Jed was a real man. There was no one like Jed – not even Mick measured up to him.

She was always glad to see Jed return to the ranch, watching for him with a yearning that was strange in a sister-brother relationship. At odd moments she had thought about the thrill of seeing him ride in, big, bronzed and totally a man, then she had shaken her head as if to throw off the confusion in her mind. Jed had always been the man in her life – her big, big brother. Strangely, she had never felt the same way about Mick. He had always been the one to pull her hair and poke her in the ribs and generally torment her when they had been kids; even now he was sometimes disparaging. Not like Jed, who always defended her.

'I've come a'courtin',' said Billy Dale doggedly.

She laughed in his face. 'Why, so you have! And now you're here what are you going to do about it?'

'Why, Rosa, what do you mean?'

'Seems to me that you should try to kiss or cuddle me,' she said with a teasing smile.

Billy Dale's face was a mask of worry and excitement. He seemed to choke. Challenged by this impish girl, he felt he had to do something. He grabbed at her arm and clumsily tried to draw her to him. Rosa laughed again. At that moment Kate Bayner walked onto the ranchhouse porch.

'What are you two playin' at?' she demanded.

Rosa giggled. 'He wants to kiss me.'

'Heck, *you* said to,' shouted Billy Dale.

'Well, you can forget that sort of thing,' Kate Bayner rapped out.

'Oh, Ma, he's old enough,' said Rosa.

Kate Bayner suddenly became angry. She pointed to the house. 'You can quit that kind of talk, Rosa. Get inside and help me . . . and Billy Dale, don't you push yourself at this girl. She ain't for you.'

'Aw, Mrs. Bayner, I've just come a'courtin'.'

'More fool you.' Kate Bayner hunted for words. 'She's too young . . . I mean . . . she don't want to be courted . . . you ain't her kind . . .'

'That sure is silly, Ma,' Rosa said. 'Of course Billy is my kind. Well, maybe he ain't big like Jed, but he does make me laugh.'

Kate Bayner got control of herself. 'I don't want you courting. Not yet. Now come and give me a hand.'

Kate Bayner kept Rosa working while Billy

Dale hung around, saying silly things and getting in the way. After the midday meal he announced that he had to ride back to the homestead.

'I've got chores to do, Rosa.'

His father had filed claim on two sections of government land about five years ago on the strength of having one son over twenty-one years of age . . . Gary Dale. So they had got the two sections, each of 160 acres, and they'd built the sod house astraddle the two parcels of land and had started ploughing, and planting corn. The only thing they kept in the way of livestock were milking cows and saddle-horses. So far the Dale family had survived, but like many more in the flatlands of Kansas they were poor. But it was a way of life for John Dale, his wife, Sarah, and their two sons. They lived in peace with the small ranchers who were not members of the Stockmen's Association. The big cattlemen in the county ignored the small ranchers and home-steaders alike and continued to wire off their big tracts of land.

'I'll ride back some of the way with you, Billy,' declared Rosa. She glanced defiantly at her mother.

Kate Bayner threw a warning look at Rosa. 'You get back here fast, my girl,'

Laughing, the two young people mounted their

horses and rode out at a fast canter. Near a fold in the land they slowed the animals. Then Rosa realized she had gone far enough. It was all of three miles back to the ranchhouse.

'I'll head back,' she said.

'I never did kiss you, Rosa,' said Billy Dale.

She laughed. 'I know you didn't. And I don't want you to!'

'Gosh, Rosa, why not?'

She was silent, inwardly perplexed. For she'd had a flashing mental picture of Jed Bayner grinning down at her, showing his fine teeth, being tall and big – the way a man should be.

As they stared at each other a rider came slowly onto the ridge behind them and halted. Billy and Rosa heard the horse's hoofs digging at soft earth and they glanced up.

The man sat rigidly in his saddle, staring, his one eye accusing. His hand came up and pointed at the girl. 'Accursed bitch, you live, while others die – but you are doomed!'

Then he broke into a wild laugh. Turning his horse, he babbled in a strange mixture of English and Kiowa phrases and rode off as mysteriously as he had arrived.

'Who's that old galoot?' Billy Dale said.

Colour draining from her face, Rosa said, 'He was riding around our house last night – in the

14

wild wind – and I saw him again this morning. Mom says she doesn't know of any man – but you saw him, Billy, didn't you? And you heard him.'

'Sure. Seemed loco to me. Who is he?'

'I don't know. He scares me. Why does he point at me?'

'I don't know. Heck, I'll ride him down, Rosa, and I'll ask him what he means by it, huh?'

'No, Billy. Maybe he's just a madman. Maybe he's dangerous. I'll ride back now, Billy. You go on home.'

'See you at the next dance,' said Billy Dale. 'That's if I don't see you before!'

She heeled her pony and went back to the ranchhouse at a fast gallop. She didn't say anything about the stranger to her mother. She knew, somehow, that she'd get nothing but evasive answers.

Kate Bayner was silent, working around the house with a grim kind of efficiency. Then she took off her apron and went outside, saying nothing to the girl. Rosa went to the window and looked out, wondering at her mother's mood. A few moments later Rosa was surprised to see her mother slowly cantering out of the ranch gates, sitting side-saddle on the slow old black mare. The girl watched her go until she was a speck on the distant ridge. Rosa turned away. The house was strangely silent, reminding her that she was alone.

Kate Bayner rode along the high ridge that gave her a view of the rolling rangeland. She saw some of their cattle in the distance; a bunch following a lead steer. She saw fleeting cloud and heard the whine of the wind that always blew across the prairie at this time of the year. There would be more whistling winds tonight, she knew. She hoped she wouldn't hear that screaming voice again.

She would tell Jed when he returned, and maybe he would know what to do. Jed was the only one she could talk to.

But maybe she could ride down on Simon Greer and treat the man to a barrage of threats and taunts, the same sort of thing he had handed out every spring to her. Maybe he would run back to his hideout in the hills; the incredible cave which was his home. He could be scared, she knew. He was loco, cunning, like an animal – and like any creature he could be frightened, even as he tried to frighten others.

For an hour she rode the ridges. Then she saw him, sitting motionless in the saddle, hunched up like a buzzard. She rode closer, down coulees and up the other side, and he would move on with a flurry of hoofs and then halt and stare at her. She

16

kept going relentlessly, trying to get within shouting distance. He circled her and waited. She rode up a grassy slope where thorn bushes provided the only cover. He reined his horse about, staring. Even from a distance she could sense the powerful glare in his one good eye.

Eventually she shouted, 'Damn you, Simon Greer! Go away! Leave us alone. You can't get your son back. He's been dead these eighteen years, you crazy fool!'

He laughed wildly and finally rode out of sight.

TWO

'Johnny Eagle
Is Beautiful'

They were coming through a shallow valley, the hills and Wichita behind them, with Winton to the south and the flatlands and home ahead. The wagon was rolling nicely with the two horses working well together. Mick was on the other side of the creaking wagon. He seemed to be asleep but that was because he'd done all the arguing and drinking he'd wanted to in Wichita. He was resting.

They had a new hand and it seemed fitting, since they were paying him wages from the time they left Wichita, that he should drive the wagon. His saddle-horse was tied to the rear of the wagon.

Jed Bayner glanced at the man and grinned. There was always a grin on Jed's lips, something that had fooled many a belligerent man who had

18

fronted him in a brawl, a cattle drive, or a saloon
– in fact, anywhere. Jed grinned at the young man
driving the team. He respected silence in a man.
And when the man was half-Indian silence was
natural. Johnny Eagle, he called himself. He was
slightly built, lithe, with long black hair. He wore
a steeple-shaped hat ornamented with a snakeskin band and impregnated with dust. His red
shirt was half-open to reveal a hairless chest. He
owned a .44 Colt in a tied-down holster. Maybe
that had been a necessary weapon in Wichita, but
there would be little use for it on a poor cattle
ranch in the middle of nowhere. There were no
rustlers and little trouble with the Kiowa. Maybe
a few unsavoury people inhabited Winton, but it
wasn't a town for gunmen.

Johnny Eagle seemed a useful hand. There had
been some trouble from Mick when Jed had
announced he was hiring the man.

'A damned half-breed!' Mick Bayner had glowered. He had a round face, like his mother, and
was of medium height. He lacked Jed's height and
wide shoulders. But he had plenty of the fighting
spirit common to both men.

'He's a useful man,' Jed had said. 'And we need
a hired hand for the first time in our lives. There'll
be work for him. We'll start branding in a few
weeks.'

'You know I don't like Indians . . .'

'He's half-white.'

'That makes it all the worse,' Mick had growled. 'Why in hell did you have to hire him behind my back? You never said a damn thing to me about it – you just up and hired him. Ain't there another man in Wichita who wants a job?'

'He's cheap. He said he'd work the first two weeks for just his keep, but I said I'd pay him.'

'That's mighty generous of you,' Mick had said sourly. 'I tell you, I don't like Kiowas.'

'Don't you remember pa saying all men were equal?'

'I don't. All I know about pa is that some swine shot him in the back. I figure it was an Indian.'

'You were only a kid at the time,' Jed had pointed out. 'For that matter, so was I. But ma will tell you the Indians had only old muskets at the time and it was a rifle that killed pa. Ma said it was a white man.'

'She don't know who killed him.'

'That's for sure. And it ain't no good talking about it now.'

'What's she gonna say when she sees Johnny Eagle?'

'She'll judge him by the work he does. That's all he's hired for.'

There had been no more argument, and they had

ridden out of town. Johnny Eagle sat on the wagon seat, calm and grave-faced. Mick had watched him for some time, then he'd apparently resigned himself to the fact that Jed always gave the orders.

At the end of the shallow valley the land lay flat to infinity. The sun broiled down. Jed looked at the fleeting cloud and wondered when it would rain. That would be a good thing – after they got the wagon and the supplies home.

They were within five miles of the ranch and the simple sod-roofed house they called home when Jed Bayner saw the movement on the ridge. They were now in rolling country, the flatland behind them.

He had seen the figure, a black shape that wheeled on a horse and dropped below the sloping ground. It was the kind of movement a rider might make if he wished to conceal himself. Wariness leaping inside him, Jed Bayner spurred his horse suddenly and guided it to the ridge. He hadn't said a word to Mick. His brother watched him curiously, walking his mount beside the wagon.

Jed Bayner saw the lone rider cantering swiftly into the distance, his thin body upright in the saddle, as if leading a cavalry charge. As he went, a wailing sound came from him; a crazy howl.

'You!' breathed Jed as he rode back to the wagon.

Mick shot him a glance. 'What was up there?'

'Just a rider . . .'

'What was he doin'?'

'He didn't say. He went off.'

'Anybody we know?'

'Nope.'

And Jed Bayner rode grim-faced all the way to the modest ranchhouse. He broke into his grin only when Rosa and her mother came running to meet them.

'Jed! Jed! Have you bought me something, Jed?' Rosa cried excitedly. She ran up to him. He had dropped from the saddle. He picked the girl up by the waist, grinning, and swung her around in a circle.

'How's my little sister?' he asked, laughing.

He set her down and went over to his mother and hugged her. 'Everything all right here?'

'Everything is all right,' said Kate Bayner.

Mick had slapped Rosa on the back and said, 'I've bought you somethin' all the way from Wichita. Boy, what a town!'

'Did you like it?'

'I sure did. I got real drunk one night.'

And then Rosa noticed Johnny Eagle sitting quietly on the wagon seat. She stared. 'Who is he?'

'That's our new hand. He's part Kiowa. Johnny Eagle is the name he goes by.'

Rosa kept on staring at the copper-skinned

young man and a red spot came to each cheek.
Johnny Eagle returned her stare, cautiously at
first, then a smile crept over his lips.

Rosa smiled. 'He's handsome, Mick, isn't he?'

Mick Bayner scowled. 'That's fool talk, Rosa,
and you know it. He's part Injun.'

She challenged him. 'Is that so terrible?' She
turned again and stared at Johnny Eagle. 'He's
beautiful . . .'

'You're talking like a fool girl!' snapped Mick.
'What's beautiful about an Injun?'

'The way he holds his head . . . something in his
face . . . oh, I don't know.'

'Don't let Jed hear you talk like this,' warned
Mick.

'Jed?' She was momentarily confused. 'But Jed
would understand. You always argue with me,
Mick. Really, if you've just came back from Wichita
just to argue with me . . .' And with her head tilted
disdainfully, she walked onto the porch.

There was work to do – unloading the wagon,
unhitching the horses and leading them to the
stable at the back of the house. The three men
attended to these chores and then went into the
ranchhouse for a solid meal. Kate Bayner had
everything ready – steaming hot potatoes and beef,
stringbeans and cabbage. This was followed with
apple pie and coffee. There wasn't much talk

around the table at first, but then the three hungry men slowed up in their eating and commented on the things they had seen in Wichita.

'Mick got drunk, Ma,' laughed Rosa. 'I bet he met a girl, too . . .'

She got a warning scowl. 'You shut up, my girl. You don't know nothin' about them Wichita girls.'

'Well, with those stores we're all set,' declared Kate Bayner. 'A good job done. We'll start branding.'

'Oh, Jed, there was a man outside the house last night,' said Rosa. 'He was screaming, yelling – and I saw him again today.'

'Rosa, don't bother Jed with that silly talk!' Kate Bayner rapped across the table.

'But he was there, Ma!'

Jed kept on grinning, showing his white teeth. 'Just some drifter, Rosa.'

'But he shouted at me. I saw him again when Billy Dale and I rode out together. He shouted some crazy things at me.'

Jed held his grin. 'Like I told you, he's a drifter, a wanderer.'

'He shouted at me in Kiowa. I'm sure it was Kiowa . . .' Mick glanced at Jed. 'What's all this about? Who is this man?'

Jed turned his attention to his apple pie and replied with a full mouth, 'Guess it's just some loco drifter. Nothin' to worry about.'

Johnny Eagle said unexpectedly, 'What did he say in Kiowa?' His voice was gentle.

Rosa looked squarely at him, seeing the regular aquiline features, the smooth, copper-coloured skin. She found herself smiling eagerly. 'I understood only the English. Oh, it's so crazy. He said I was accursed.'

Mick put his spoon down. 'If I meet up with this galoot, I'll shut his damned mouth. Accursed? What the hell does he—?'

Kate Bayner cut in, 'Please, Mick, I won't have swearing at the table. Your pa never did that, and you ain't gonna start.'

The meal was over and soon the men went out to do some more chores. Jed showed Johnny Eagle the ranch buildings – a stable, an earth-floored shack which had stalls for two milking cows, the horse corral, and another sod-house which served as a tackroom. When he had pointed to the distant boundaries of the spread and a group of cows on a grass slope about a third of a mile away, Jed went into the house to see his mother.

'Rosa saw him,' he said grimly.

'He was outside the house last night, screaming his loco threats.' She wiped her hands on her apron. 'Then she saw him again down at the creek early this morning. He – he shouted at her, Jed.'

'Simon Greer.' He breathed the name like a curse.

'I saw him as we rode back, Ma. He was riding that damned horse like he had a poker in his back.'

'I can't stand any more of it,' Kate Bayner whispered. 'Every year since you were little . . . he just rides around this house. One day Rosa might understand his loco talk, or some family in Winton will dig it all up and point the finger. Maybe somebody will start to believe the things Simon Greer says.'

'No – everyone figures he's loco – and he is. Nobody takes any notice of him, Ma.'

'But some remember him when his son was alive, when he had a wife and a section of land and wasn't mad.'

'He's mad now.'

'But what can we tell Mick? Oh, I wish I'd confided in Mick when I told you everything, Jed. But Mick always seemed so young. Or maybe it was because you always seemed strong, Jed, even as a boy.'

'Leave it to me. I'll hunt around tonight. I'll give that mad old devil somethin' to cackle about – if he's still around, that is.'

'He'll be around. It's the anniversary of his baby son's death. God, it's been eighteen years since the Kiowa killed the child. He—'

'Don't you upset yourself any more, Ma,' Jed interrupted.

26

When the sun had dropped over the horizon like a red ball of fire, Jed Bayner went out and saddled his horse again. He wore a leather coat buttoned across a black shirt. He pulled his fawn stetson down over his forehead because the wind was rising again. He had a sixgun in his holster and a rifle in the saddle scabbard. Maybe he'd need them. Maybe he should kill Simon Greer. No one would miss the damned nuisance. If he lay in a gully for a week, the buzzards would see that only a skeleton would remain. The man was like a bug in a blanket. He was a nuisance, but maybe some day he'd get to be dangerous.

Jed didn't say anything to anyone when he left the house, but Rosa saw him ride into the cold night and turned to her mother.

'Where is Jed going at this time of night?'

'Just taking a look around.' She kept her eyes down.

Mick frowned, went to the window and watched his brother disappear into the lighter shadows of the moonlit night. Johnny Eagle was sitting straight in a chair, watching Rosa.

Jed Bayner went around the ranchhouse searching thorn bushes and anywhere else a man might hide. All the time the wind increased in velocity until he had to lean against it, his horse making frightened noises. He kept a firm rein on the animal, jigging it forward. He was three-quarters of a mile away from the ranchhouse and had completed the circle when he suddenly saw the lean dark shape sitting high on his horse. Jed nudged his mount into a canter, and at that moment the elusive shape ahead seemed to disappear. But there was a scream from a human throat that blended with the whining wind.

'Accursed . . . accursed! A-yaka a-gumba.'

The wind suddenly howled like a twister, tearing the madman's scream into the night and raising a small sandstorm. Jed reached the spot where the man had been but there was no sign of him. The night had swallowed him. Dust swirled in devilish circles, blotting out visibility beyond ten yards. Jed moved on, hoping to blunder into the man. He felt the urge to kill. If he saw the shape of the loco man, he would fire his sixgun. It was how he felt at the moment. He had heard the Kiowa words: 'A-yaka a-gumba.' He knew what they meant and he damned Simon Greer.

At the end of an hour he had to ride back home. He rode the horse into the stable, unsaddled it and wiped it down. Then he tramped back to the house, lifted the latch and went in.

'Just where have you been in this blasted wind?' demanded Mick.

'Lookin' around.'

28

'For what?'

'Thought I'd see that galoot who scared Rosa.'

'Now why'n hell should he be around on this cold night?'

'He might. I figured to send him packing.'

'That's a crazy reason for goin' out in that damned wind,' said Mick. 'Set yourself down near the fire, man. We've had a hard day.'

Jed grinned. His mother's round face was wide-eyed and pale. Rosa, wearing a long cotton dress, looked lovely sitting there with her embroidery work. And Johnny Eagle seemed quite happy to sit and watch the others. Jed saw him looking at Rosa.

Night came and it was peaceful. Then there was a day of work, with the new hand riding out with Jed to start a count of new calves. It was a hard but good day. It seemed that Simon Greer with his mad fantasies had vanished back to the cave in the hills. But during the afternoon of the second day, when all three men, along with Rosa and Kate Bayner, were busy inside the ranchyard fence, there was movement in the distance.

A small party of Kiowa braves was slowly riding towards the ranch. The leader wore a solitary feather. He was a big man, naked from the waist up. There were four Indians and they held rifles. Blankets showed colourfully on the black and white ponies. The riders came on and halted two hundred yards from the ranchhouse.

'What are they doin' down here?' demanded Mick.

'I wouldn't know. It's been a long time since we had any Kiowas around here,' said Jed. 'They've stuck to their land in the foothills for many a year.'

'Kiowa, huh?' muttered Mick. 'We got one right here, in our house.'

His comment wasn't heard by anyone except Jed. He stared at the four braves. 'Get Rosa and ma back into the house.'

'Surely they ain't gonna attack?' said Mick. 'There ain't been Injun trouble for years.'

'Just do as I say, Mick. Get Rosa and ma back in the house.'

Mick started to escort the two women to the house. As Rosa walked back, one of the braves pointed. It was a slow, deliberate movement. His arm was held rigid for what seemed a long time and then slowly it dropped.

Johnny Eagle was behind Jed. 'They've come only to look.'

'What makes you think that?'

The half-breed shrugged. 'I know, that is all. They look. They will be here a long time.'

There were no shouts from the Indians, threatening moves. They simply sat and watched the ranchhouse while the sun blazed hotly on their backs.

It was Mick who broke the spell. He came out, grumbling, close behind Jed. 'Look, I'll put a bullet close to them ponies and maybe that'll make 'em get.' Mick held a rifle. 'They give me the creeps just sittin' out there on those horses. What's the idea anyway?'

'I don't know, and neither do you. Just keep that rifle pointed at the ground.'

Suddenly, the Indians wheeled their ponies around and rode off in a cloud of dust.

Jed and Mick watched them until they vanished down a fold in the land. 'Gone,' said Jed. 'Now what the hell brought them here?'

Mick could only shrug.

The next day, before the midday meal was ready, Billy Dale rode over on his big chestnut. He slid down from the saddle and ran up to Rosa as she came out of the ranch house. She had seen his approach from a window. Billy went right up to the girl and put a clumsy arm around her waist. 'I'm a'courtin',' he announced. 'Pa says I can come a'courtin', Rosa. He says he don't mind a bit – not if the gal is you, Rosa.'

'Hey!' She struggled out of his grasp. 'Who says I want you to, anyway?'

'You didn't say no the last time,' he spluttered. His mouth hung open slackly.

'Billy, what will Jed say?'

Red Hide

'Jed . . .? Reckon he'll pat me on the back when he hears I've got permission to come a'courtin'.'

Rosa looked around, wondering if Jed was watching. He had been in the house only a few minutes ago. If he was watching, maybe she could make him jealous if she let Billy Dale snuggle close, maybe Jed would get real annoyed. Then she frowned. What in heaven's name was she thinking about? There was no sense in making Jed jealous. He was her brother. Yet something nagged at her. She allowed Billy to hold her. He was shaking with excitement. He tried to kiss her, but she moved her head. In that second she saw her mother on the porch, glaring angrily at her. And in the doorway of the house stood Jed.

His face was set like a mask. He stared at her with hard eyes.

Confused and knowing she was a foolish girl, she ran from Billy Dale. She went around the house and stood against the clay bricks, breathing hard.

Billy Dale rode off when Rosa wouldn't speak to him. But he got only as far as the rocks that marked the trail to Winton. Then the Indians came and shot him dead. He fell into a gully and his horse ran off. The four Kiowas thundered into the distance, flat against their ponies' manes.

THREE

The Stranger
In Town

A grieving father picked up Billy Dale's body and slung it over a horse. John Dale turned on Jed, his face twisted with anguish.

'He wouldn't be dead if it wasn't for that sister of yours . . .'

It was the day after Billy had been killed. John Dale and his son Gary had come over to the Bayner ranch to see why Billy hadn't returned home. They had spotted his horse moving uncertainly about a shallow dip in the grassland and from then on it was just a matter of searching. When they found the body they discovered it had been scalped. There were four bullet wounds.

'Rosa can't be blamed for this,' snapped Jed Rayner.

'No?' For a moment John Dale buried his face against the body of his younger son and then he jerked around and glared at Jed. 'I've heard tales in Winton. I know what that loco wanderer says . . .'

'Simon Greer?'

John Dale was hunched in his worn tweed coat. He looked suddenly tired, like a man who'd done too much work and had nothing to show for it. 'Yeah, Greer. He's been in Winton, you know, mouthing his fool talk. I never took much notice myself, but now . . .'

'There ain't no damned buts,' snarled Jed. 'He's a raving maniac.'

'Well, it's Indians who killed Billy . . .'

'So? They're Kiowas on a rampage, although I don't understand why. There's been no trouble for years.'

'Why'd they kill Billy?' said Gary Dale suddenly. 'What did he do to them? They had no reason. They even scalped him! What's got into those damned Kiowas?'

'That girl,' mumbled John Dale.

Jed turned fiercely. 'You've got no right to say that, Dale.'

'Well, that loco Greer says —'

'I don't give a damn what he says!'

Gary looked at his father. 'What's all this about

34

Greer? What're you talkin' about, Pa?'

'It goes a long way back . . .'

'Well, tell me.'

'Just shut your fool yap, John Dale!' Jed warned. 'I'm not having Rosa talked about. And nothing that crazy old bastard says makes sense. He's been loco since he lost his son.'

'Sure. The Kiowas killed the baby in cold blood. He wasn't even a year old.'

'Hell, it's an old, old yarn,' argued Jed. 'In those days the Indians raided and fought, robbed and attacked. In fact, it's only in the last eight or nine years that they've learned to live and let live. God almighty, Greer should forget what happened eighteen years ago.'

'But he can't.'

'That's why he's crazy,' shouted Jed. 'And anyone who takes any notice of him is a fool.'

John Dale put out a hand and gently patted the dead body slung over the horse. 'He was a good boy. Just young and wantin' to go see a gal. I didn't mind – I'd forgotten the things old man Greer said . . . and now I ain't so sure. Kiowas killed Billy and—'

'Shut up!' cried Jed Bayner. 'You say it and I'll punch a hole in you, Dale.'

Gary Dale went up to Jed and glared. 'You won't touch my pa.' He stood close, eyes blazing. He wasn't as tall as Jed Bayner and not as wide-shouldered. He wore a plaid coat and a flat-topped hat. He wasn't armed, for a homesteader's son didn't carry a gun like a gunslinger. 'I aim to get to the bottom of this. What's all this about Rosa, anyway? And Greer? Hell, if I see that man I'll talk to him. Maybe I'll get to know myself what this is all about.'

'You'll be listening to a madman.'

With a scowl Gary Dale walked back to his horse and took the leathers. 'Well, this yap isn't getting us anywhere. But Billy is dead, so I'll wear a gun in the future and the next Kiowa I see, I'll drop.'

'Then you'll have the troopers after you.'

'Yeah? Well, I sure hope the army goes after the savages who killed Billy.'

'Report it to the law in Winton,' said Jed tersely. 'It's a job for the Indian agent up in the Kiowa hills and the army boys.'

There was nothing they could do but take the body back to the homestead. Then they reported to the sheriff in Winton.

Jed had to tell his mother how they had found Billy Dale. He found her alone in the house.

'He's dead, Ma. Scalped.'

'Kiowas?' she said incredulously.

'Something is wrong,' he said grimly. 'Something

made that bunch of braves come to the ranch and stare like they had never seen whites before. Those Indians must have killed Billy, but John Dale is blaming Rosa. He mentioned Simon Greer, but I stopped him dead in front of Gary.'

Kate Bayner put her hands to her face. 'There's going to be trouble,' she moaned. 'Trouble . . . I can feel it . . . and Simon Greer is behind it all. I wish he was dead.'

Jed slapped his sixgun. 'Any more loco talk from that damned nuisance and he will be dead.'

Mick and Rosa had heard Jed's horse return. Now they walked into the ranchhouse with questioning looks.

'Billy Dale is dead,' Jed told them. 'We found him in a gully . . .' He outlined the rest of it but said nothing concerning John Dale's remarks about Rosa. The bare truth was enough. Kiowas had killed the youth for no apparent reason. And, worse, they had scalped him, something that had not been done in these parts for a long time.

'Scalped him?' gritted Mick. 'Kiowas! But why? What had he done? What could the Indians possibly have against him?'

Rosa was horrified. She watched her mother turn away with a sad face, and said, 'Oh, poor Billy! They killed him. And he came to see me. Savages!'

'That's true,' said Mick grimly. 'I don't like

37

Injuns. Damned Kiowas. And now we've got one right here in our house.'

He saw Jed look at him queerly. Then Jed said, 'If you're referring to Johnny Eagle, I've told you he's half-white.'

'And that's a bad mixture,' flared Mick.

Jed and his mother exchanged glances, then Kate Bayner said, 'Well, the troopers will visit the Kiowa settlement and maybe find the killers.'

Mick went to the window and stared out, wiping a fresh trickle of sweat from his brow. 'Why did they kill him? Jed, remember how that party of braves came to the ranch the other day?'

'I'm remembering.'

'First time I've seen anythin' like that for years.'

'Well, don't worry too much about it.' Jed grinned again, although there was little amusement in his heart. 'Let's get back to work.'

It was a day later that Jed told his mother, Mick and Rosa that he was riding over to Winton to see if anything was being done by the law about Billy's death. He added that he might call at the Dale homestead on the way. 'You keep an eye open, Mick. Wear a gun.' Jed paused. He wished he could confide in Mick totally but somehow the present moment seemed wrong. He wanted to tell his brother to shoot on sight if he saw Simon

Greer. But Mick knew nothing about the man. Mick had not been told the family secret – and it seemed impossible to tell him. But he did say, 'Watch out for the Kiowas. Don't start shooting unless you figure there's trouble. Anyway, I'll be back tonight. And don't let Rosa go too far from the ranchhouse.'

'Why don't you take Johnny Eagle back with you and pay him off?' asked Mick. 'I don't need a part-Kiowa around here.'

'He stays,' snapped Jed. 'He's a good worker. Cut out that fool talk. Johnny Eagle is all right.'

Jed Bayner rode out. He had made an early start. The wind was cool and the sun had yet to warm the land. After riding a mile or two at a canter, he let his animal walk. At that moment he decided to visit the Dale homestead.

The Dale property was only a few miles out of Winton. A few trees grew at the back of the sod-house, the only timber for miles around. There was a fence around most of the homestead, a makeshift barrier of wire and posts. It would keep off a wandering steer, but that was about all.

John Dale was repairing a primitive plough. He stopped work as Jed rode through the open gateway in the fence. 'You can stop there,' Dale said.

'You don't sound too friendly.'

'I ain't. Billy is buried over there.' And John

39

Dale pointed at the back of the house. 'All on account of a gal who—'

'You stop it!' warned Jed Bayner.

The other man glared. 'You know the truth about your sister. If she is your sister . . .'

'She is.'

'Well, you know – and so does your mother . . .'

Jed held his patience. 'I just called to ask if there's any news about what the law is gonna do about the Kiowas.'

'Gary rode into Winton yesterday and told the sheriff. He's gettin' in touch with the Indian agent. But that sure as hell won't bring Billy back.'

'I'm riding into Winton myself, to tell the sheriff our side of what happened to Billy.'

'You can do what you like, Jed Bayner. But don't come back here. I've been thinking about the tales that loco Greer spins. Well, maybe there's some truth in them. Gary is gonna make it his business to find out. He and Billy were real close. Now look at me – I've only got one son to work this land.'

The man complained in a harsh monotone. Irritated, Jed wheeled his mount around and rode away from the nester.

Some time later he entered Winton, a quiet town that would never be as big as Wichita. The place lay on the plain, a one-street town with a

40

rutted trail leading in, and another track leading out to Wichita. There was a scarcity of timber around Winton and so most of the buildings were of adobe, with a few solitary homes on the outskirts made of sod and rock.

Jed Bayner went to the small wood and stone building that was the sheriff's office. It was square in shape with a single cell tacked on as if as an afterthought. The sheriff, Art Kortner, was laboriously writing a letter with a quill pen as Jed entered.

'What do you want?' he asked.

'What's happening about Billy Dale?'

'I sent a man over to see the Indian agent on the Kiowa reservation. It's his business, and maybe the troopers'.'

'It might be months before the army has any men to spare.'

Art Kortner nodded. 'Might be at that. Then it might not. There's trouble brewing. Not many people know this at the moment, but it'll soon get around. The Kiowas in the hills have complained to the Indian agent that some of their men and women have been murdered. Scalped.'

Jed frowned. 'It's news to me, Sheriff. I don't quite understand. Who would scalp an Indian except maybe another brave from a different tribe?'

The other man's pale blue eyes flicked nervously. 'It ain't Indians. I know who's causing the trouble. They rode into this town three days ago after a spell in the hills and the flatlands. A bunch of hired hardcases led by a man called Downey Hollister. Ever heard of him?'

'No. Who is he?'

Art Kortner got up, walked across the office and stopped at a map of the territory. 'He's come up from the south, from Tulsa. But I ain't tellin' you any more, Bayner. It's a matter for the law and the troopers. Now you just get back to your land and cows.'

'Wait a minute. Billy Dale was a friend of ours. Seems to me his death ties in with the death of the Kiowas. I'd like to know more.'

'Not from me. We've had Simon Greer in town today and he's been mouthing off about your sister. I told him to get, and stop stirring up trouble.'

'He's the trouble-maker. He's been riding around our house at night singing crazy songs and scaring Rosa.'

Art Kortner tugged at his leather vest. 'That's not against the law. I can't bother myself with some loco gent, not when I can smell big trouble.'

The sheriff wandered around his office, grunting. A question about Downey Hollister brought a snarl from the lawman. 'He's a hater. You'd better keep away from him. He's a man of wealth and he hires gunmen. I got information about him from the telegraph office in Wichita. He's trouble. Now git, Bayner, and stick to your cattle. Billy Dale is dead and you can't do anythin' about it. Just look after your family.'

Another question brought a wave of the hand from the sheriff. It was a dismissal. The man didn't want to talk. So Jed Bayner went out, collected his horse and walked it down the main street. A sense of belligerence stirred in him. He had been warned off Hollister. For that reason alone he would seek out the man, speak to him and assess him.

FOUR
Grim Trophies

There was only one real hotel in Winton. The building of clapboard and brick stood on a corner and was known as Greg's Hotel, the name of the owner. With the only saloon directly opposite, the two establishments provided a focal point in the town. Not far away was a bank. Close at hand was Wilson's Mercantile, a store that sold everything. But Jed was interested only in the hotel at the moment. He had been told that Downey Hollister was staying there.

But the nervous little hotel clerk informed him that Hollister did not want to see anyone; he was resting. Jed crossed the road to the saloon and bought a beer. He was not really a drinking man and he only knew a few men in the place. He nodded to two and then looked casually at a group

44

of three men who had 'gunman' stamped indelibly on their faces.

One man, the smallest of the three and barely more than twenty, owned a pair of matching Colts in cutaway, thonged-down holsters. The other two wore single guns. They grinned as they spoke, but there wasn't much amusement showing in their cynical eyes.

Jed Bayner didn't need a blueprint to know that these men could only be Hollister's hard-cases. There were two questions in Jed's mind: what were these men doing in a placid town like Winton, and why did a man called Hollister employ them?

Any man with sense didn't tangle with this kind of rannigan if he could help it. Jed kept his eyes off them for a long time, then he became alert when he heard one of them say, 'I'm gonna take the saddle-bags off my horse. Keep that bottle of rotgut on the bar. I'll be back in two minutes.'

Jed finished his drink a second later and strolled away. He remembered Art Kortner's words, 'It ain't Injuns . . . I know who's causing the trouble . . . a bunch of hardcases led by a man called Downey Hollister. He's a hater . . .'

Curious, he left the saloon, then paused on the boardwalk and saw the tall, lean gunslinger walk down an alley at the side of the saloon building.

There was a livery stable at the bottom of the alley; a walk of only about twenty yards. He waited and saw the man disappear into the livery. A bit later the gunman walked swiftly back again. He barely flicked a glance at Jed Bayner.

Minutes later, Jed sauntered down the alley to the livery to have a look at the horses belonging to the hardcases. A man could learn a lot from horses. There might be brand marks or scars. Being able to identify a horse could be a useful detail.

The place was not locked and the old hostler was nowhere in sight. Jed walked into the small livery and moved slowly down the line of horses in the stalls. There were five animals in all. He thought one belonged to a Winton man; he had seen it before. The other four must be the mounts of the hardcases. One of the horses caught his attention. It was a big magnificent grey with a wicked eye. The horse was saddled. Initials were carved in the leather and painted with gilt. D.H. The saddle was fairly new and had scrollwork on both sides. Downey Hollister! Evidently the man wanted only the best in horseflesh and saddlery. There were two saddle-bags. For a man who was resting, he wasn't giving his horse much relief. Or maybe he intended to ride out soon. Whatever the reason, the animal was saddled and ready for use at a moment's notice. Jed glanced at the other horses again. One was saddled. He looked around. Scuffed leather saddle-bags hung from a nail in a stall post. The bags bulged. Evidently these were the saddle-bags the lean man had decided to hang up.

Jed touched the leather. Suddenly he unbuckled the strap and flipped open a bag. He stared at the contents for a long time. Then, distaste lining his features, he slowly picked out something.

A human scalp.

He held the trophy of long black hair. The skin and flesh had dried up. He figured the scalp was a week old – and Indian. And the bag held at least seven of these grisly objects.

Jed Bayner went over to the big grey and ran his fingers over the scroll on the saddle. D.H. The boss-man. Maybe look inside his saddle-bags would be a good Idea.

It was no surprise to Jed when he saw the same horrible objects that had made the first bag bulge. Scalps. The two saddle-bags on the big grey were stuffed with stiff pieces of skin, blood, flesh and long, lank hair. He didn't bother to count.

He walked from the livery, taking care that the bags were strapped down before he left. He went straight to the sheriff's office and walked in. Seething with anger, he leaned on Art Kortner's desk. The man's pale blue eyes flickered uncertainly as they met Jed's challenging gaze.

'I tried to see Hollister,' Jed said.

'I told you to mind your own business.'

'It is my business. Billy Dale was killed and scalped by Kiowas. It's all my business.'

'Hollister is a dangerous man. The army will take care of him.'

'When they get around to it. He wouldn't see me at Greg's Hotel. He was resting.'

'Just as well, Bayner. He's got hired guns.'

'I know. I've just seen them in the saloon. I've been lookin' at their horses in the livery.'

'You'll stop a slug, Bayner. Keep away from those men.'

'There's enough evidence in their saddle-bags right now to hang all of them,' flared Jed. 'Go take a look, Kortner. Do your job. You'll find enough Indian scalps there to incriminate the hardcases and their boss-man. They've been hunting Kiowas – killing and scalping. That's why Billy Dale was killed. If something isn't done, there'll be a lot more folks killed.'

'I told you I sent a man over to see the Indian agent.'

Jed thumped the desk. 'You can do something now. Get a posse and arrest Hollister. I'll back you up.'

'Men will die!' The bitter comment was flung at Jed. 'Could be me – or you – anybody. I know something about these men – and about Hollister. I told you he was a hater. He's a bit mad, I think, and he hates all Indians. I told you I got information about him – he's been tied in with Indian killings, but nothing has been pinned on him so far.'

'Now's the chance. He's carrying bags full of evidence. Let's go get him. Grab a gun, man!'

'You think I want to die for blasted Indians?' Art Kortner's voice climbed into a falsetto. 'I'm sheriff of Winton, not the whole country. These Indian hunters broke no laws here. Anyway, I've told you the Indian agent has been informed. He'll get the army.'

'You'd allow murderers to ride in and out of Winton?' asked Jed incredulously. 'What the hell are you wearin' that badge for?'

'The Kiowas are the business of the Indian agent and the army.'

'But Billy Dale was murdered by the Kiowas – right here on your doorstep practically.'

'Yeah. Well, maybe that was different. He'd been to see your sister, and she—'

'You repeat that goddamned talk of Simon Greer's and I'll punch your head in,' warned Jed.

Art Kortner got clumsily to his feet and moved

around angrily. 'All right, you just tell me the truth about that girl.'

'You can go to hell. I don't have to tell you anything.'

The sheriff pointed to the door. 'Then get to blazes out of here and go back to your place. The army can take care of Hollister. It ain't your affair and it ain't a job for me. I'm not as young as I used to be and I don't figure to get filled with lead by Hollister's men. I guess they'll move on, anyway. They'll just up and move.'

Jed grinned mockingly at the other man. 'They might move on – to kill more Kiowas – and that will send the Indians out to take more revenge. You've got trouble, Kortner. You can't just shut your eyes to it.'

But the sheriff merely shrugged. The man just hoped the trouble would ride away, out of Winton, out of his area. He'd leave it to the army to handle Hollister and take care of the Indian trouble. Art Kortner just wanted to patrol the peaceful street of Winton and no more.

Jed Bayner left the office and stood on the boardwalk, his face grim. Then he decided to march into Greg's Hotel and haul out Downey Hollister. He re-entered the hotel and walked past the little clerk to push into the hotel lounge. It was a small room with three leather chairs and a mahogany table on which lay old copies of a news-paper printed in Wichita. Hollister wasn't there. Jed went out to the stairs and climbed them two at a time as the little clerk at the reception cubby-hole emitted protesting little squeaks. Jed barely heard him. He reached the landing and moved along it. If Hollister was resting, he was going to be disturbed.

Jed opened two doors and looked into empty rooms. He found one door locked and he thumped it with a blow that strained a panel. He moved to the next door and banged on that. He didn't know how many guests were staying at Greg's Hotel or how many were in their rooms and he didn't care. If he made enough noise he would surely discover Downey Hollister.

He found the man. A door opened and a polished Colt poked out to point at Jed's chest. Jed grinned, apparently unperturbed.

'You Downey Hollister?'

A head of silver grey hair nodded as cold eyes assessed the intruder. Hollister was big and wide-chested. His handsome silk shirt strained over barrel-shaped ribs. He straightened, balancing himself on the balls of his feet, the gun steady in his hand.

'My name is Hollister. So who the hell are you? Why all the noise?'

'You don't like Indians,' Jed rapped out.

'What's it to you?'

'Could be plenty. I see by the contents of your saddle-bags that you've been killing and scalping. Are you crazy? It's a crime these days to murder Indians. They've got a reservation and they live under the law's protection.'

Hollister's eyes suddenly glittered. He stepped into the passage and Jed saw that his left arm hung lifelessly. The fingers were curled up, as if the sinews had died. The hand was a useless claw.

'You've been snooping. I've killed men for less than that.' Hollister raised his gun slightly.

'You must like blood,' said Jed. 'And scalps. Kind of dirty, ain't it, carrying black-haired scalps around? What does it do for you?'

Downey Hollister said, 'I could kill you right now.' His eyes were unnatural; they glittered too much. Jed had stabbed at some sensitive spot deep in the man's soul. 'Just who are you, mister?'

'Jed Bayner. I run cattle on a spread fourteen miles out of here and I don't like what you're doing. I'm nearer to the Kiowas than anybody in Winton. So I'm askin' you to take your hate thing a long way from here.'

Hollister said coldly, 'You're a fool. Few men talk to me like that, but I'll give you a chance. Git!'

The man's gun moved, but Jed didn't budge.

'Scalps. It's dirty. What's the obsession?'

'I told you to git!'

'It has to be something mad. White men don't scalp.'

'You're wrong,' Hollister said. 'There was a time when an Indian scalp was paid for. That was in the days when the only good Indian was a dead one. Trappers made money on scalps. The army paid for 'em – even wagon train bosses would pay for 'em.'

'That was a long time ago,' Jed said.

'It was a good idea then and it's a good idea now.'

'But the Kiowas are peaceful. It's murder.'

Suddenly the gun jabbed at the man's useless left arm, then whipped back to cover Jed.

'Indians did this to me. All because of some stinking redskins I walk around a one-armed man. Every night I look at my withered arm and I swear revenge.' Hollister took a deep breath. 'God, I don't know why I'm telling you this! Now, for the last time . . . git!'

'No, Hollister. We don't want crazy bastards like you around – so *you* can git. Take your filthy scalps with you before somebody stuffs them down your throat.'

Hollister's throat swelled with rage. His thick grey hair danced as he jerked his head. It was a signal for three men to come up quickly behind Jed Bayner. He turned, hearing the swift, light footsteps. Fists rammed and thudded against Jed's head and body. His fists went up instinctively as he staggered under the onslaught.

'Get him, men!' snarled Hollister. 'Beat the daylights out of him! Beat him to pulp!'

FIVE

The Raving Accusations

There was no way Jed could avoid the punishment the three hardcases handed out. Punches came fast and furious and there were kicks that rammed painfully into his shins and ribs. A fist dug mercilessly into his mouth. Another thumped low into his groin. Jed flailed away. He punched a man's jaw and then another's ribs. The two men who were hit moved back. Jed punched out again and his fists landed dully against an arm, a chest. Then someone kicked him from behind. He twisted around, trying to get his back against the passage wall. It was the man with the twin guns who was kicking. Jed had to use his feet as well as his hands with this kind of opposition and he hacked

55

out at the young hireling and had the satisfaction of hearing him yell in pain when a boot got his knee. But this fast, furious retaliation took his attention away from the other two men and the result was thudding blows that landed brutally against his face. Jed felt blood spurt from split lips and one eye flashed violent lights back to his brain. He reeled. Another kick got to his groin. Jed slid down the wall and tried to block more blows. But a punch rammed into his mouth again, then a numbness came. He fell to the floor and rolled over, face against the threadbare carpet that ran down the centre of the passage. He lay there for a few moments and the three hired toughs took turns to kick at his ribs. With each kick Jed's body jerked. He didn't lose consciousness and something in the blackness of his dazed mind urged him to try and escape the torture. He crawled on the floor. The men began to laugh.

'Kick him to death!' snarled Hollister from his room doorway. 'He's an interfering bastard!'

From the start of the beating, the little clerk downstairs had heard enough to send him scuttling to the sheriff's office.

Then Art Kortner was there in the passage and he had to do something. He stared at the grinning hirelings who were standing around and getting set to take more kicks at their v.ctim.

56

'Cut it out!' barked the sheriff with all the authority he could muster.

The three hardcases laughed and flashed glances at their boss as if asking for instructions.

'Do as the lawman says,' sneered Downey Hollister. 'Let this bastard go. Maybe he's learned a lesson.'

Art Kortner swallowed with difficulty before venturing to speak again. Then, 'This is a peaceful town. What's all this about?'

'This man came to my room and threatened me,' said Hollister. 'I don't know why – maybe some loco idea stirring him – so my men came to throw him out. That's it, Sheriff.' He smiled and turned away. His three men grinned, looking down at Jed Bayner. One spat at him. The young man toed Jed speculatively and then looked at Art Kortner.

'Next time it'll be guns,' he said. 'And he'll die.'

Jed got to his feet and swayed, wiped his mouth and stared at the sheriff. Then, incredibly, he grinned. 'Sheriff, you're just the man I need. I charge these four men with possession of Indian scalps. They're murderers – wholesale killers. You'll find the evidence in their saddle-bags.'

Art Kortner dragged in his breath. His face was pale. 'Why don't you shut up, Bayner? Hell, do you want to get us both killed?'

Jed leaned against the wall and nodded at the little clerk, then he transferred his gaze to Downey Hollister. 'The army will hang you some day. Right now I suggest that you get to hell out of this territory. You're trouble. You're stirring up the Kiowas.'

Hollister snarled at Jed. 'You're asking to be cut down, Bayner. No man talks to me like you're doing.'

Jed's eyes glinted angrily. 'All right, I'll take on you dirty, blood-stained carrion one at a time.'

Kortner grasped Jed's arm. 'Come on, let's git.'

Sanity returned to Jed. He didn't want to die. He was prepared to fight any of them, but the odds had to be better than this. So he limped along the passageway with Art Kortner and went down the stairs. Then he was in the street. He'd lost his hat, but it was an old battered relic and didn't matter.

'You did fine, Sheriff,' he said. 'Thanks.'

'I advised you to ride home.'

'I wanted to see Hollister. He's an Indian hater.'

'I know that. It's no secret.'

'Let's go around to the livery stable and pick up those saddle-bags and the scalps as evidence. Then, when the army arrives you'll have something to show them. I'll make out a deposition . . .'

Art Kortner looked uncertain. 'I don't know . . .'

58

Red Hide

At that moment the three hardcases came out of the hotel and walked to the alley that led to the livery, throwing mocking glances at Jed and the sheriff. They trudged along, their hardware swinging with every stride. The youngest one, the two-gun fellow, walked as if the town was his.

'There goes your idea about getting the saddlebags,' said the Sheriff.

'You seem kind of relieved.'

Art Kortner pointed towards the yellowed trail that the passage of horses, wagons and stage had worn into the earth. 'Git, Bayner. If you know what's good for you ... git! Those hellions will ride on. Sooner or later they'll mean nothin' to Winton – or to you.'

Jed kept on grinning. 'Your notion of upholding the law is kind of quaint, Sheriff. They'll ride, sure – on another Indian hunt.'

Kortner turned and walked away.

Jed went to his horse, clutched the pommel and lifted himself to leather. He sat and glowered. The scalp-hunting would end if Hollister died. The gunhands only worked for money. Hollister was the man with the hate.

Jed walked his mount down the main street. The daily stage was ready to leave for Wichita. People stood around the depot. A wagon was being loaded at the freight office and the pair of mules

59

looked like they'd never move. The ring of hammer on metal sounded from the blacksmith's and two boys played in a horse trough, splashing each other.

He had to make a decision. Maybe he should leave the whole affair for another day at least. Maybe the Indian agent would get the army to inquire into the death of Billy Dale and pacify the Kiowas over the death of their kin – and at the same time pick up Hollister and his trio of killers.

It was a big maybe because the army was occupied elsewhere. In fact, the nearest troopers were over fifty miles away in the wooded hills looking for five deserters who had fled with an army payroll. How quickly they would return to base depended upon luck. But maybe some men could be spared if the Indian agent made enough noise.

Jed Bayner rode out of town. He had told the family he'd be back that night. He'd stick to that.

He little realized that just before sundown that day, long after he had quit Winton, a man with a ramrod-straight back rode into town and glared at everything with his one good eye. He had no real reason for being there. In fact, Simon Greer had no reason for doing many things except eat and sleep and sing his mad songs. But Winton was a place he went to whenever he left his cave in the distant hills. He knew he'd be allowed to stable his horse, and he could sleep in the straw near the animal. And there were men in the saloon who'd buy him beer and laugh at his crazy talk. So he rode in, hitched his mount to a tie-rail and lounged on the boardwalk, his back to the wall. At intervals he would break into a babble of incoherent speech. Then he would be silent and stare sternly at nothing. Few people bothered to listen to him. He was loco. His talk was mainly about the Kiowas and his son. The torrent of insane chatter barely made sense. In other territories it was crazy talk about gold that characterized lonely old madmen. With Simon Greer it was Indians – and his lost son. Mixed with all this senseless gibberish there was the mention of a girl.

'Rose Bayner!' he suddenly shouted. 'Accursed! A-yaka a-gumba!' He glared. A man walked past, grinning. Simon Greer shook his fist. 'Doomed bitch! Others die! A-yaka a-gumba!' He glared again. 'My son ... those dirty savages ... my son ...'

A man who was closing his small store for the night became tired of the crazy figure on the other side of the street. He pointed to the hills. 'Get to hell back there, you mad old fool. Shut up your damned bawling. You never had a son. You're Indian crazy, that's all.'

'My son!' howled Simon Greer. 'Curse you, Rosa Bayner! A-yaka a-gumba.'

'Ah, shaddup, you loco drifter!' snarled another man. 'Go some other place and make noise.'

A man in a new white Stetson and a beautifully cut doeskin coat over an immaculate silk shirt paused on his way to Greg's Hotel. A long cigar was between his lips. He stared keenly at Simon Greer and listened to the crazy chatter. He took the cigar from his mouth and blew smoke, then he buttoned his coat and adjusted his hat. He did all this with his right hand. His left hand hung like a withered claw.

'Who the hell is that?' Downey Hollister asked the storekeeper.

'Him? That's the loco gent, Simon Greer. He's crazy and a blamed nuisance . ... '

'I can see he's crazy,' said Hollister. 'What was that he said there about Rosa Bayner? Did I hear right?'

'You did. Always yapping about his son and the Kiowas and that gal . . .

'Rosa Bayner?'

'Yeah. Always the same. I never take any notice usually – but this time he's getting on my damn nerves.'

'Bayner . . . that name sounds familiar. Who is she?' The storekeeper took another look at the man's expensive clothes and decided that he might be a future customer. So he expanded. 'She lives with her family on a small ranch that goes by the brand Double O.'

'Is that big feller, Jed Bayner, any relation?'

'That's her brother. There's the mother, Kate, and a brother called Mick. They come into town every so often.'

'Jed Bayner has just been in,' said Hollister. 'And he's a man I won't forget.' He fingered his chin and stared at Simon Greer. 'One-eyed and mad! But for the grace of God, there we go, sir.'

'I don't get you. I – I beg your pardon . . .' stammered the storekeeper.

'We're all slightly mad, my man.' Downey Hollister touched his dead arm. 'Maybe you should take pity on this madman.'

'He's a damn nuisance,' said the storekeeper.

'A-yaka a-gumba,' muttered Downey Hollister. 'Do you know what that means?'

'Can't say I do. Makes no sense to me.'

'It's Indian talk.'

'Yeah? Well, that figures. Simon Greer is Indian-crazy.'

'Is that a crime?' snarled Hollister.

The storekeeper backed away. 'I – I dunno.'

'A-yaka a-gumba,' said Hollister again. 'It's Kiowa. I know plenty of Indian phrases –

Cheyenne and Kiowa – it's a kind of hobby of mine.'

'You don't say,' said the storekeeper.

Simon Greer suddenly pointed and shrieked. 'Rosa Bayner! A-yaka a-gumba.'

'Mighty interesting,' said Hollister. 'A-yaka a-gumba. It means an Indian bastard. You say this girl is Jed Bayner's sister?'

'Sure. A nice gal.'

'Bayner is no Indian. How come?'

'I don't know . . .' Backing away again, the storekeeper decided to mind his own business because of the glitter in the stranger's eyes. 'I guess I don't really know much about the Bayners . . .' And he darted back into his store. Downey Hollister crossed the street and touched Simon Greer on the shoulder. 'You can come along with me. I'll buy you a drink.' Hollister stared at the man's one good eye. 'You like drink, don't you? A beer, maybe a whisky?'

A residue of reason lay low in the demented man's brain. His own speech was incoherent but he could make sense out of other people's statements. He nodded and said, 'A drink? Sure.' Then his mouth twisted and his one eye rolled fiercely. 'Accursed bitch . . . my son . . . there'll be doom . . . doom . . .'

He accompanied Hollister to the saloon where

he consumed whisky greedily. At intervals he would burst into a fierce torrent of words, often mentioning Rosa Bayner. There wasn't one clear sentence, but the pile-up of angry, repetitious phrases was enough for Downey Hollister. He ignored the few men in the saloon who laughed as he plied Simon Greer with drink. Hollister listened, and when he had heard enough he escorted the crazed man to the darkened street outside and handed him some money.

Then Hollister returned to his hotel room where he sat down to do some thinking. He spent most of the night in solitary thought, separating grains of fact from Simon Greer's ravings.

SIX

The Indian Hater

The family was glad to see him return. Kate Bayner gave him a hug and Rosa laughed and took his arm as they stood on the porch. But Mick was proddy.

'That damned Johnny Eagle. He gave me some lip.'

'What about?'

'I told him he'd have to bunk somewhere else – maybe the barn.'

Jed said, 'There's a spare bedroom for him in the house.'

'He's a Kiowa.'

'Only half. I keep telling you, Mick. He's half-white – not that it matters to me what the hell blood he owns to.'

'I don't like Kiowas – or any damned Indians,

for that matter,' snapped Mick. 'You know that. I think you ought to consider my opinions, Jed, and quit pushing everything down my throat just because you're older. If I don't want a half-breed in the house I've got a right to say so. You—'

Mick cut his talk because Rosa came back to the porch and stood close to Jed. She saw Mick's angry face. His body was taut, his hands on his hips, his shirt sleeves rolled up.

'Oh, you two, arguing again,' she said. 'What on earth is it all about?'

'Nothing you need worry about, Rosa,' said Jed.

Mick flared again. 'Why can't you speak out to Rosa? She knows an Indian when she sees one. Why do you have to figure it ain't her problem? She's got plenty of sense. She'll understand what I'm saying.'

Jed tried to grin. 'Mick wants Johnny Eagle to keep out of the ranchhouse.'

'Oh? Why? What's wrong?'

'Johnny Eagle happens to be half-Kiowa.'

Rosa turned to Mick. 'That doesn't mean a thing.'

He was furious at having to explain his prejudices. 'You know how I feel about Indians, Rosa. I just think he should bunk somewhere else. I told him that this morning and he gave me some lip.'

Jed's eyes narrowed. 'What exactly did he say to you?'

Red Hide

'Ah, something about you hiring him, so you'd tell him where to bunk. It was the way he said it . . .'

'You're imagining things,' said Jed quietly. 'He stays in the ranchhouse. We haven't got a separate bunkhouse.'

Over a late meal which the two women prepared, Jed was asked about his visit to the Dale homestead. 'How are they taking it?' asked Kate Bayner.

'Badly.' Jed forked a potato. 'They've buried him. Gary Dale has been to Winton to see the sheriff. He's contacted the Indian agent and maybe he'll get in touch with the army. And that's it.' Jed kept silent about Downey Hollister and his evil collection of scalps. It would only arouse Mick. And it was something Rosa shouldn't hear about. Besides, news of that sort would only worry his mother.

Later that night, with the others gathered around a log fire, Jed stood on the porch and watched the full moon throw shadows beyond the house. He listened to the noises of the night, including the bellowing of steers. He was thinking about Hollister and his terrible hatred. He wondered if the man would ride away and leave the Kiowas to settle down again. Maybe Art Kortner was right in one sense, but it was a cowardly way to look at it.

68

He half-turned when Rosa came out to join him. He grinned at her.

'It's a nice night,' she whispered. She looked closely at his face. 'You didn't explain that you were in a fight. Those cuts – and you've got the makings of a black eye.'

'It was just some galoot in a bar.'

'Really, Jed! What on earth were you fighting about?'

'Nothing really.'

She held his arm. 'Jed, you're lying. Men don't fight about nothing. But never mind – I don't expect you to tell me everything.' She looked at the dark, deep vista of the land for some moments. 'The plains are so big, aren't they, Jed? Mile after mile before the land rises into the hills. It's kind of lonely, yet I love the sense of limitless freedom. Even the hills . . . You know, Jed, sometimes I have a strange yearning for the hills. It's as if I want to go there and, well, stay there. Isn't that odd?'

He ran his hand through his thick hair. 'I can understand it. A lot of us get a yearning for the land . . .'

'But this is so real. I – I sometimes think I must have been born in the hills.'

'You were born right here, Rosa. We've had two new sod roofs since then, so I've been told. But this has always been your home.'

'You're so good to me, Jed.' She studied his face and then suddenly she put a hand to his cheek. A moment later, acting on an impulse she couldn't understand, she kissed him. It was a meeting of lips and the touch was so electrifying that she jerked her head back and stared.

'Jed! I . . .'

She thought he was angry. His features were tightly lined. For a long time he didn't move. He searched her eyes, her face. His hands were on her shoulders. His face came a bit closer to hers and then he checked the movement. He licked lips that were suddenly dry.

'Rosa, I – I'll always take care of you.' He paused. 'No one will hurt you.'

She laughed shakily. 'Who would want to hurt me, Jed?'

'There are people who – who hate,' he muttered.

'But I don't hate anyone. Of course, I don't meet many folks, except at the dances at Winton – and that's only once a month. But I don't hate anyone, so why should they hate me?'

'There are folks who know nothing but hate.' He broke away from that subject. 'I'll take you to the next dance in Winton. It's a cattlemen's affair and maybe you'll need a new dress.'

'Oh, won't that be nice.' Her brown eyes were shining and she was still very close to him. Her attitude was natural; he was Jed, the big brother she adored, the man she was always eager to see. She hugged him. When she drew back she was startled to see the strained expression in his eyes. There was a twist to his mouth. She sensed his stiffness, the queer way he was looking at her.

'What's the matter, Jed?'

'Nothing. What makes you think—'

'Shouldn't I touch you?'

His reply seemed to grate from deep in his throat. 'Rosa, maybe I ought to tell you something . . . maybe I should have told you this years ago. Or ma should have spoken . . . but . . . she wouldn't let me . . .'

'Jed, what are you trying to say?'

He looked away. Then he took her hand. 'Little Rosa – so lovely. No man will ever hurt you.'

Just to be so near him, to feel his hand on hers, produced such strange emotions in her that she felt confused. Jed was her brother, a wonderful man, the sort a girl ought to have for her own. It was a staggering thought. She shouldn't think like that. It wasn't right. Not about Jed . . .

'Jed, maybe we should go inside,' she whispered.

'But there's something I should tell you. Maybe the time has come . . . and maybe it'll be better for both of us . . .'

But he didn't get around to telling her the truth

that night. A man's cry came from out of the darkness. His voice was thick with hate.

'You damned red hide! You'll die! We'll take your blasted scalp, you stinking little red-hide bitch. Just see if we don't!'

Jed leaped down from the porch and slammed a hand to his hip. But he wasn't wearing a gun that night. He glared angrily into the darkness. There was moonlight but he couldn't see the man who'd shouted the threats.

Rosa cried, 'Who is it, Jed? What does it mean?'

Again the voice came: 'You dirty Kiowa bitch! You've been fooling people long enough. I know all about you. You're going to die, red hide! I'm makin' it my business to see you die. We want your long, black-haired scalp.'

Jed Bayner raced back into the house to get the rifle. He rushed out again. Rosa was against the wall of the house, her hand to her mouth, fear stamped on her face. In the moonlight she looked pale. Jed tore past her, rushed to the pole fence and vaulted it. He ran into the night, wondering where the man was. If he found him, he would kill him for frightening Rosa.

He knew who was out there. Hollister. He recognized the voice, even though it was thick with hate. Hollister. So Hollister had learned a lot in the past few hours. Who had he talked to?

The man was crazy with hate – almost as bad as Simon Greer but in a more menacing, deadlier way.

Simon Greer . . . Had Hollister met the madman? Then Jed was running in a circle, his rifle at the ready.

Hollister had to have a horse somewhere. The land was flat Kansas prairie but even in flatland there were folds and hollows. Hollister had to be somewhere in a hollow, maybe lying flat on his belly. But Jed remembered that the man was a gunhand. It would be stupid to run into a bullet. Jed halted, wishing the man would shout his threats again. If he did, he'd die.

But as Jed stood searching the night for a sign of movement, there were running footsteps behind him and he wheeled.

It was Mick, gun in hand. 'What the hell goes on, Jed?'

His elder brother gritted his teeth as he searched his mind for a reply. This was hardly the time or place to attempt explanation of a subject that had existed for years without Mick knowing about it. He snapped, 'Some damned intruder, Mick.'

'Is it the drifter who scared Rosa?'

'Could be.' Jed's lips tightened. Grimly, he realized the time was coming when he would have to tell Mick the whole story. That would raise a lot of problems, knowing Mick.

The distant sounds of hoofs suddenly drummed through the night. The horse was a long way off. Try as he might, Jed couldn't see a shape. The man had kept his horse hitched a fair distance from the ranchhouse, out of sight.

'The blasted pest has gone,' Jed muttered.

'What the hell was he shouting about?' asked Mick. 'I didn't quite catch it – but I heard somethin' about red hide. Now what in thunder does that mean?'

'How would I know?' Jed said. He was irritated. Rosa had heard the shouts and would have questions. How could he answer them? He said, 'Let's go into the house.'

'Can't even hear hoofbeats now,' Mick said.

They reached the porch and Rosa came forward. 'Oh, Jed, what does it mean? That terrible man was shouting about *me*!'

'No. It's just some crazy fool.'

Rosa shook her head, her long black hair blowing across her face. She looked pale in spite of her tan. 'I heard everything he said, Jed.'

'Pay no attention,' he told her. 'Guess it's that crazy drifter who scared you earlier.'

'It wasn't, Jed. The voice was different. It was a much deeper voice – and full of an awful hate.'

Jed took her arm and took her into the house. He closed the door and placed the cross-bar in the sockets. When he turned, Kate Bayner was watching him, her face filled with fear. She didn't dare ask Jed any questions, not with Mick, Rose and Johnny Eagle close to hand.

When they were seated in the big living room and Jed had stirred the fire, Rosa pressed on with her fearful questions:

'I heard that blaring voice, Jed, and the man said something about Kiowa bitch – and red hide – and fooling people long enough . . .'

Jed Bayner straightened and said through compressed lips, 'Take no notice. It was just some crazy fool. It doesn't make sense.'

'But it must have *some* meaning.' Rosa looked at her mother and at Jed. She saw fear in her mother's face and she noted the hard set to Jed's jaw. 'Jed, he was shouting about me – like that other crazy man – the one-eyed man.'

'Who the devil is that?' snapped Mick. 'Who are you talkin' about?'

'The man who shouted at me when I was with Billy Dale.'

'He's loco,' said Mick slowly. 'He's the crazy galoot who comes into Winton now and then. I've seen him maybe twice, but I never took much notice of him. Is that the man who frightened you, Rosa?'

'Yes – twice,' Rosa 'said. 'But the man who snarled those terrible things just ten minutes ago isn't the same man.'

'There are two of 'em?' Mick growled. 'You heard him better than me, Rosa. What did he say exactly?'

'Something about a Kiowa bitch . . . and he said he wanted a scalp . . .'

'That don't make any sense,' Mick said.

Jed punched the palm of his hand. 'Let's forget it and go to bed. I might go into Winton tomorrow.'

Mick turned abruptly and shot Jed a glance. 'If you do, I'll go with you.'

'Why? There's work to do here.'

'Why are you figuring to go to Winton then? If you go, I'll ride with you.'

'All right,' Jed said. 'If I go to Winton you can mosey along with me.' Anything to shut Mick up seemed good enough. If there was any talking to be done, any truths to reveal, any other time was better than right now in this house where everyone was on edge. And he'd take a gun tomorrow. It was becoming increasingly obvious that Hollister had to be stopped.

Jed hustled his mother to the room she shared with Rosa, and Mick went into the bedroom he shared with Jed. When they left the living room, Johnny Eagle smiled gently at Rosa, then he reached out to touch her long black hair. It was an innocent and tender movement.

'You are a beautiful girl, Rosa Bayner,' Johnny

Eagle said simply. 'You are like a scarlet flower in yellow soil.' He turned away to go to his room, a cubby-hole built on under the roof. As he went he muttered softly in Kiowa, 'As I have known from the moment I first saw you, you are a full-blooded Indian. *A-saba ugh uja.* I will love you.'

But no one heard him. He disappeared into his room. Rosa watched him go, smiling as any girl might at the compliment he had paid her.

There was no more talk. Kate Bayner went to bed and pretended to sleep, so Rosa had to content herself with her confused thoughts.

Jed roughly waved aside any comment from Mick and dropped onto his bunk, turning his back on his brother. Johnny Eagle walked around his small room for some time. He was stripped to the waist and wore only his pants and socks. His skin gleamed like polished bronze in the light from his small lamp. Once he paused and smoothed the skin on his arm and stared at it.

'Red hide,' he muttered. 'I am more red than you, Rosa Bayner, and I am only half Kiowa. But I know . . .'

The next day Jed Bayner was up at first light. The sound of him moving around awakened Kate Bayner and she dressed and got up and came to the kitchen where Jed was pumping water. He grinned at his mother.

77

'I've washed. You want some water, Ma?'

'I want to talk. Quickly, while she's still asleep. That man last night – who is he? You know him, don't you?'

'Yes.' There was no point in stalling now. He had thought it out. He'd have to tell her. 'He's a man called Hollister, an Indian-hater. He's a kind of sadist.' And he told his mother all that had happened in Winton. 'My guess is that the Kiowas killed Billy Dale in revenge. He just happened to be there. But John Dale is connecting the little he knows about Rosa and blaming her . . .'

'How can he make sense out of that?'

'It's illogical, sure. But Indians killed Billy, and he suspects that Rosa is—'

'You needn't say it, Jed,' Kate whispered. 'She's your sister.'

'Ma, you know and I know that isn't true. And I've got to tell you that Rosa means more to me than a sister.'

Kate Bayner's eyes widened and she shook her head helplessly. 'No! That's not right. She's your sister. I've brought you up as a family – you, Mick and Rosa. Don't say such things, Jed. It ain't right! You can't – you can't—'

'It's got to be faced sooner or later.'

'No! I won't have it!' Her voice was emphatic, almost desperate. 'She's my little girl – my Rosa. I

78

brought her up – best part of it alone – after your pa died. She's your sister, Jed. You can't talk like that – I won't stand for it.'

He knew there was a fantasy working in his mother's mind. Long ago she'd decided not to face up to the truth. Only once had she faced reality and that was when things were bad and there was drought in the land and cattle were dying. They had stayed up one night, talking about the hardships. He had been little more than an overgrown boy, but he was working fourteen hours a day and more, digging for water and burying cows when they were found dead. She had felt able to confide in Jed that night. She had told him the story of Rosa. Simply, without trimmings, she had spoken of many things. That night Jed got the truth and accepted it because he had a young mind and was free from prejudice. But Mick had been too young, so he hadn't been told. And then fantasy had returned to Kate Bayner. Never again did she talk to Jed about the night she found Rosa and buried her own child. Now and then, when Simon Greer appeared, raving in the night, she spoke to Jed and cursed Greer and his dead son. It was only during the time of these fears that she spoke to Jed about Rosa. At other times, Rosa Bayner was her daughter – and Jed's sister.

There was no more opportunity for Jed to speak

to his mother about the things on his mind, for Mick came into the kitchen then, followed soon after by Rosa. She wore a simple gingham dress that hugged her slender waist and revealed the swell of her high, proud breasts.

Ten minutes after eating, Mick found Jed in the stable tightening the cinch on his saddle. There was a rifle in the saddle scabbard and Jed had his gunbelt strapped around his waist.

'You goin' to town?' Mick asked.

'Yup.'

'I'm coming, too. You've got something on your mind. I want to know what it is. And you can tell me why that galoot last night was yellin' about red hides. I figure you know more than you're letting on, Jed.'

'Maybe he was shouting at Johnny Eagle.'

'Don't try to fool me,' Mick said sharply. 'He said somethin' about Kiowa bitch. That don't make sense but—'

'Saddle your horse,' Jed interrupted. 'And bring a gun.'

'If you're going to tell me what it's about, you can start now.'

'The hell I will, Mick! You'll play it my way.'

'Yeah? Well, what happens if the Indians mosey up here like the dirty snakes they are and figure to do more than just look at the ranch house while we're gone? There'll only be that 'breed to defend ma and Rosa. He's half Injun. He won't fight his own kind.'

'You hate Indians, don't you?' Jed grabbed his brother's shoulders and the grip was so fierce that Mick grimaced.

'That's true. I don't like 'em. Don't ask me to explain why. I can smell a redskin a mile away and they're no good.'

Jed Bayner's rage flared. He punched Mick between the eyes. Mick staggered and then fell to the stable floor. He jumped up, raised his fists and glared at Jed.

'What the hell was that for? Just because I said somethin' about Indians? What's got into you, Jed?'

'You and your stupid talk about smelling a redskin a mile away. I won't have that kind of talk around here.'

'But why? Plenty of others talk like that. Are you defendin' that damn 'breed, Johnny Eagle?'

'Look, quit your yap. It's time you dropped this dislike of the Kiowas. Just accept that they exist. You'd better watch it, Mick; or you'll become one of those twisted. Indian haters. Now get your horse and a gun. Maybe we'll have a talk on the way . . .'

For some minutes Mick Bayner worked in

81

silence, saddling his horse and throwing angry glances at his brother. Then he led his horse out, returned to the house for his gun belt and strapped it on. His mother watched him fearfully.

Some time later, when the two men climbed into their saddles, Rosa and Kate watched from the porch.

'Do you have to go to Winton again?' Rosa asked. 'Why, Jed? What is it all about?'

'Just some business to deal with.'

'You and Mick? Are you going after that man who shouted last night?'

'Don't concern yourself about it, Rosa.'

Kate Bayner just stood there with tight lips, deep concern in her eyes. Then Johnny Eagle came riding up. He had been over the flatlands to a waterhole that had long needed cleaning. He smiled at Rosa and looked inquiringly at Jed Bayner.

'You just hang around, Johnny, and look after ma and Rosa,' Jed instructed.

'Sure, I'll do that.' Johnny Eagle smiled again at Rosa.

'Watch for the Kiowas,' Mick said.

'They won't bother us.'

'No? Well, those savages did kill Billy Dale . . .'

'Come on, Mick,' Jed said.

They went off at a canter.

Johnny Eagle found jobs to do around the house.

He would obey orders. It suited him. He wanted to be near Rosa Bayner. He wanted to watch her and admire her graceful movements. Just to look at her supple form fed his need for someone like her. He had never known anyone as lovely as this dark, lithe girl. He marvelled that others did not guess the secret. He had only to look at her to know.

Some miles away from the ranch, Mick demanded: 'You can start giving me some facts. I think you know who shouted those crazy things last night.'

'I do.'

'Well? I'm listening . . . and I want answers.'

Jed drew in a deep breath. 'He's called Downey Hollister. He's a crazy Indian hater.'

'Well, what's that to us?'

'I'm going to kill him – exterminate him before he causes more trouble.'

'Why? Because he hates Indians?'

'He and his three gunslingers have been killing and scalping Kiowas,' gritted Jed. 'He's got a rep all the way from Tulsa. He's mad. He's stirred up the Kiowas and they killed Billy Dale in revenge.'

'Well, the army can deal with this Hollister.'

'We can't wait. After last night you can take it from me that Hollister wants to kill Rosa – and then scalp her. You want to know why?'

Mick stared. 'I sure do.'

SEVEN

'Get Out Of This, Cowman!'

The two grim-faced brothers talked plenty on the trail into town, and once Mick Bayner nearly turned his horse and left Jed.

'I can't believe it,' he snarled.

'You've got to. Rosa ain't your true sister. Or mine – for which I'm glad. She's a full-blooded Kiowa.'

'You're tryin' to get me mad,' Mick ground out. 'You're just sayin' this because you know how I feel about Indians.'

'Don't talk so damn crazy! Do I look like someone mouthin' off just for the hell of it? Listen to me, brother. Rosa is an Indian. Ma picked her up one night – with pa – when her own baby girl died suddenly. It all happened on the one day . . . the baby died . . . choked on something . . . there

84

wasn't even time to get a doctor. Then, that night, they heard the sounds of a fight out on the flat-land. They knew there were Indians out there. They went out on horseback to investigate and found the Indian camp burned to the ground. Some troopers had taken revenge on the redmen . . . killed all the women and children and the old men except for one baby that was hidden under some rocks. Ma insisted on taking the Indian child home. It was a baby girl. Ma kept the child . . .'

'Rosa?' said Mick hoarsely. 'Not Rosa?'

'Yes. The Kiowas in the hills didn't know anything about it for a long time – until Simon Greer's son was captured by them.'

'Greer? The loco galoot?'

'Yes, only he wasn't crazy then from what I've been told. The Indians were pretty active in those days, and they attacked Greer's wife one day when she was driving a rig. They left her badly wounded and took the baby boy. A bit later they tried to barter the boy for Rosa . . .'

'They knew she was an Indian?'

'That's right. They wanted to swap the two infants. Ma just wouldn't listen to it. By then she had got to thinking that Rosa was her own.'

'That was stupid,' Mick grunted out.

Jed glared at him. 'Yeah? You listen to me, brother. She was grieving for a dead child. You

85

wouldn't know what that was like. And neither would I. So she refused to swap the baby. After a week the Kiowas killed Greer's baby son. He blamed our family for that. He went mad with sorrow and never really recovered. His wife died later and he took to wandering, always returning here, raving about his son and the Indians.'

'Didn't people listen to him?'

'Some, maybe. But that was eighteen years ago. Many of those people are dead now. Others have forgotten the tale. Many never believed it, even at the time. The whole thing is shrouded in the past and vague rumour – and it should stay forgotten.'

'Ma never told me the truth,' said Mick bitterly. 'Why? Why in hell wasn't I told?'

'She always figured to tell you. But then you got this dislike of Indians.'

'She told you.'

'One night, when she was sorely troubled. After that she spoke of it only when Simon Greer came with his mad singing and babbling.'

They talked like they were strangers. Jed watched Mick keenly as they rode along. Would Mick change his views about the Kiowas?

Mick sat his horse for a long time, hunched, haggard-faced, throwing out bitter comments. Then a challenge flared from him:

'It don't alter my opinion about the Kiowas. But

Rosa – I just can't take that right now. As for the Indians, well, I don't give a damn for 'em and never will.'

'You'll accept Rosa as our sister?'

'Maybe.' After a pause, Mick added, 'I can't believe it. Rosa, my kid sister – a full-blooded squaw!' The last word was spat out.

'You can shut your mouth on that kind of talk,' Jed barked. 'I warn you – I'll bust you one every time I hear you give out with that clap-trap.'

They entered Winton and slowly made their way down the main street to Greg's Hotel.

'This snake, Hollister?' Mick said. 'A scalp hunter?'

'Yes. That was him last night, bellowing his fool head off.'

'I heard some of his crazy talk.'

'He wants to scalp Rosa.' Jed watched Mick's face as he said this.

'Bastard!' Mick muttered.

'That's how I feel,' said Jed.

But Mick flared again, turning in the saddle. 'I'm the one who's been fooled. Both of you – ma and you – fooling me!'

'Please forget it, Mick. I've told you how it happened.'

'What if this Hollister talks? Maybe he'll tell the sheriff – the storekeepers – everybody. The whole damned town and territory will know – and sneer. Everybody ain't so friendly towards Indians as you, Jed. We'll be laughed at.'

'Look, Greer jabbered for years but few folks listened to him – and even fewer still believed him.'

'Hollister ain't Simon Greer. He hasn't got the same madness.'

'He's insane, believe me.'

'Maybe, but only on the subject of Injuns, from what you tell me. Folks will listen to *him*.'

Jed got down from the saddle. 'They won't have time. He'll be dead.'

Mick said in a savage whisper, 'You can't just kill a man.'

'He's dangerous. He intends to kill Rosa – scalp her like an Indian.'

'You've just told me she is an Indian.' Mick's voice held distaste.

'Watch your damn tongue! Do you figure to have your sister butchered?'

'My sister . . .' sneered Mick.

Jed grabbed his vest. 'Are you with me or not?'

'I'm with you but only because you're my brother.'

'All right. Listen. Hollister has three gun-slingers, one of 'em is a young feller who packs a pair of matching Colts. All three are dangerous.

88

Sheriff Kortner doesn't want to make a move against them. He hopes they'll just ride on – or the army will appear and take charge of the situation.'

'Maybe Art Kortner's right . . .'

Jed looked at the hotel windows, tight lines etched in his face. 'We can't wait for the army. Apart from stirring up the Kiowas, Hollister might carry out his threat against Rosa at any time.'

Mick was silent.

They walked into the hotel. Mick trailed behind his brother, suddenly unsure, lacking Jed's savage mood. Jed got the desk clerk's attention and asked, 'Where is Downey Hollister? Is he in his room?'

'They've gone. All of them, thank goodness.'

'Hollister and his men?'

The man nodded. 'They checked out today. I believe they rode out of town. Such dangerous men – but you know that, sir.'

'Where did they head? Have you got any idea where they've gone?'

The little man stuttered out, 'How – how should I know? All I can tell you is they checked out of this hotel. They saddled horses and rode out of town. Maybe the sheriff knows where they headed.'

In the street, Mick turned on Jed. 'What if these

hardcases are ridin' to the Double O?'

Jed tugged at the reins of his horse, leading the animal along as he strode out. 'We'll see Kortner. Just a few words, then we'll head back.'

In the sheriff's office, Jed said, 'We had Hollister at our place last night.'

Art Kortner quit stirring his morning coffee. 'Hollister? What happened? Why'd he ride all that way?'

'On account of his hate,' Jed threw back. 'His Indian hate. Can you tell me where he's gone?'

'He didn't bother to tell me,' said the sheriff. 'He headed out with his three sidekicks. I trailed them past the town limits and all I can tell you is they headed west.'

'That's the direction of our spread!' Jed exclaimed. 'But we saw no sign of them as we rode into town.'

'A man also rides west to get to the Kiowas,' Kortner pointed out.

'For more scalps? Don't you see how dangerous this man is, Sheriff?'

'I'm still waitin' for news about the army.'

'How long do you figure to wait?'

'You expect me to arrest four gunslingers?' Art Kortner cried out, then his coffee-stirring hand jerked badly and nearly upset the mug.

'I've got it figured out,' Jed said. 'Kill Hollister

and the others will ride clear. They work for money, not hate.'

'If you pick a fight with Hollister,' gritted Kortner, 'make sure you've got witnesses to prove it was a fair fight. That's if you survive.'

Jed moved to the office door. 'We're goin'.'

'Just one more thing,' said the sheriff.

'What's that?'

'They took that crazy man, Simon Greer, with 'em. He went helling out like he was leading a cavalry charge, straight-backed, fist waving and singing a wild song.'

'So Hollister did talk to Greer.'

Kortner looked down at his coffee. 'Beats me why they want him taggin' along. The last I saw of 'em, only Hollister seemed happy about the set-up. The other three had sneers a mile wide on their faces.'

Back in the street, Mick had a comment to make as they vaulted into their saddles. 'We made a bad play coming here. Hollister could be riding to the spread – and I don't expect Johnny Eagle to lift a finger. He's a 'breed. He'll run.'

'There you go again,' Jed rapped out angrily. 'Johnny Eagle has guts and he packs a gun. But there's something queer about this. If Hollister was headin' straight for the Double O, we'd have cut his trail coming into town. We saw nothin' –

not even a single rider in that direction.'

The two men left town in a fast tattoo of hoofs and took to the west trail. They went fast for a few miles and then had to decide whether to veer towards Kiowa territory or head for their own ranch. The land stretched flat as far as the eye could see, merging into a bluish tint with the horizon and the distant hills that marked the area of the Kiowa reservation. Except for dips and hollows and some small furrows that scarred the ground, there was no place where a man could hide. It was a land of prairie grass, now yellowing slightly with the sun.

Jed figured it out. 'You head back home, Mick – just in case Hollister has a plan to hurt Rosa. I'll go forward in a wide loop and see if I can pick up sign of that bunch.'

'And then what? You aim to take on four gunmen?' yelled Mick.

Jed showed his white teeth. 'Nope. Just one man – if I sight him and can separate him from the others.'

'It's damned risky. Those men could be anywhere.'

'I know that. I won't waste any time. I'll head back home as fast as this horse will take me. In the meantime, you get to the ranch and protect Rosa. Johnny Eagle will help you.'

Mick grated, 'A half-breed and a —'

'You say what's on your mind and I'll bust you one,' warned Jed.

They parted, horses jigging, then turning and tearing into a fast lope.

Jed kept his horse panting and blowing for some miles and then he let the animal slow down. While plodding along he saw three wandering Indian ponies. They eased out of a small hollow in single file, heads nodding.

Three riderless horses; he didn't need more pointers to know what had happened, not with men like Downey Hollister and his bunch at large. Jed urged his horse back into a canter. The three ponies wheeled in fright and took off with a thud of hoofs, running in a wide circle across the grassland.

He came to the hollow and hauled in his mount. He sat high in the saddle, looking down at the three bodies sprawled in the depression. Three buckskin-clad Indians were dead. One lay on his back, two bullet wounds in his chest. Another corpse, on its side, had spilled blood over grass and stones. The third body was huddled in a grotesque sprawl as if agony had kinked his muscles just before death. All had been scalped.

So this was why Hollister had ridden out of town. He must have known he would find the party of Indians somewhere in the area. Maybe someone riding into town had reported seeing the Indians. But where was Hollister now? Had he made a detour? Why had he taken Greer with him?

Jed Bayner turned his horse. He could do nothing for the three dead Indians, not even bury them.

As Jed pulled his horse's head around he became aware that he'd ridden into a trap. Four men rose from another depression in the ground, a short distance away. They held rifles at waist level.

Jed Bayner stared as the horses in the depression struggled to their feet. They had been pulled down and kept down, flat on their sides, because the dip in the earth wasn't deep enough to conceal a standing animal. Now the men came forward, grinning.

'Thought I'd run into you again, Bayner.' The taunt in Hollister's voice was tinged with contempt. 'You're not so smart, cowman.'

Jed decided that he'd die taking at least one of the killers with him – and Hollister would be the first to feel a brain-tearing slug. But first he'd answer taunt with taunt.

'You're mad, Hollister. The army will string you up. And also your men – that's if I don't kill you

94

first!'

'You will like hell!' The sneer aroused rumbling fury in Jed's guts. Hollister followed it with a derisive laugh. 'How do you figure to get out of this, cowman?'

'I'll kill you and die happy.'

'Yeah? I figure you'll be gut-punctured before you can get that hogleg clear of leather. That's my bet, cowman.'

On the face of it, Hollister was right. Jed was staring at four rifles. He'd need unbelievable luck even to pump one slug with accuracy before a shattering barrage tore into his body.

Hollister smiled, holding his gun easily with his one good hand. The other three were beginning to look restless. One said, 'All right, when do we blast him, boss?'

Swiftly, Jed rapped out a taunt: 'Where d'you aim to sell your scalps, Hollister? You're fifty years out of date, man! You belong to the past – to the raging Indian wars.'

'You've got a slack mouth, Bayner.' The other man rose to the bait. 'That red hide so-called sister of yours makes you an Injun-lover. Well, I don't like that. And I don't like you, Bayner. You're big, stupid – and you've bucked me. You —'

'I've got two good arms.' Jed's leer was designed to infuriate. Anything was better than sitting high in a saddle and providing a target for hot lead. 'That's better than you, isn't it, Hollister? Two good arms, man!'

'We'll topple him in one second flat,' said the young gunman. 'I'll even take him on myself in a draw. That Colt of his ain't no killer gun.' The young gunman lowered his rifle, ready to exchange it for his matched sixguns.

But Hollister was staring piercingly at Jed Bayner, hate bubbling in his eyes. 'By God, a bullet is too quick for you, Injun man. You—!'

'You're mad as well as being only half a man,' sneered Jed.

'You'll suffer, Bayner! You'll—!'

'Do we blast him, boss?' asked a gunman.

'No. We'll kill him bit by bit – the way the rotten Injuns would do it. Then we'll ride and get that red hide bitch and teach her she ain't no white woman before she dies and we take her scalp.'

'You're the boss-man,' said the youngest man. He relaxed and looked at Jed with the curiosity of a man who wonders how another man will die.

'You'll all die before you get anywhere near Rosa,' Jed cried.

'Redskin bitch!' spat Hollister. 'Imagine it – passing herself off as a white gal – the dirty little Injun squaw.'

Jed nearly leaped at the man. But he let the

impulse freeze. He flattened his buttocks hard against the saddle. It was queer, but Hollister's vicious invective seemed a signal, for a man rose from the hollow where the horses had been held flat and stalked forward. His one eye blazed at Jed Bayner. His spine was unnaturally straight, rigid. He walked on, yelling madly:

'That accursed bitch . . . my son . . . my son . . . dead . . . because of that accursed bitch . . . a-yaka a-gumba . . .'

'Hell, do we have to listen to that?' said one gunman, turning his head slightly

'Let him rave,' said Hollister. 'He's waited a long time for revenge. I guess he's entitled to mouth off a bit. His son was white.'

'Yeah, but—'

'He was white!' shouted Hollister. The Kiowas killed the kid – and that Indian papoose was brought up as white.'

'Maybe the old fool is right about all that – but it was sure a long time ago – and he's crazy, sure thing. Maybe he never had a son.'

'I believe him,' said Downey Hollister. 'And what I believe you'd better take as gospel.'

'You're the boss. You pay.' There was a slight sneer in the answer, as if to indicate that nothing mattered except loot.

'He goes along with us to see that squaw get her

come-uppance. I'll show this old feller just how to deal with a squaw that's got the damn nerve to live as a white woman.'

The gunman moved his rifle impatiently. The muzzle stabbed at Jed. 'And him? Come on, Mr. Hollister, what do you aim to do with *him*?'

'We can cut the sinews in his left arm . . . slice it to ribbons . . . and maybe the other one, too, for good measure. And then we can let him crawl for the rest of the day. We'll come back to put a bullet in his skull.'

EIGHT

The Killing Starts

Mick Bayner came down the well-defined track that led to the Double O ranch and eased his blowing horse. He was home and everything seemed in order. He could hear Johnny Eagle sawing fence posts, and Rosa was singing an old love song, loud and clear. She was in a happy mood, it seemed. A grin started and then faded. Rosa! God, it was a new Rosa he had to face.

He'd been fed lies. His mother had lied all these years, but she had confided in Jed. For him – only lies!

He got down from the horse and walked it to the corral. He was opening the corral gate when Johnny Eagle appeared. The man was wearing only pants. His chest was wet with sweat. The sight of the hairless chest infuriated Mick Bayner. He also noted that Johnny Eagle had his long hair tied at the back like a pigtail, Indian style. He wore his gun. He was taking his role of guardian seriously, Mick thought.

'Where is Jed?' asked Johnny Eagle.

'Do you mean Mr Bayner?' Mick said nastily.

'Sure, anything you say. Is he staying in Winton?'

'What's it to you? Matter of fact, he's on his way here. Now take my horse and rub him down. Put some work into it.'

'I'll do that,' said Johnny Eagle quietly. 'It's no hardship.'

Tight-lipped, Mick stared after the man, almost wishing he'd start an argument. Then he turned and tramped towards the house.

It seemed his mother was always cooking or washing or cleaning up the house. She got down from a wooden chair on which she had been standing. 'This sod-roof! I wish we had a timber and shingle roof, like some of the places in town. The insects we get! I've been cleaning in the bedrooms. Grasshoppers and beetles! We'll have to stand the bed-legs in bowls of kerosene if this goes on. We—' She broke off sharply. 'Where's Jed? You didn't stay long in Winton. What happened?'

'Nothin' happened.'

Kate Bayner wet her lips. 'Did – did you find that man who came here yelling last night?'

Mick gritted his teeth. 'We got a clue.' He didn't know what else to say. There was a barrier between himself and his mother. He felt he could only talk to her if he lost his temper. If that happened, everything would be spat out. Maybe it *should* happen.

As he stared, Rosa walked out of the kitchen, wiping her hands on an old dish cloth. She smiled at Mick. 'Back? Where's Jed? What did you find out in town? Did you meet up with that awful bellowing maniac?'

It seemed that for the first time he noticed the darkness of her long, brushed hair and the coppery hue of her skin. He'd always thought Rosa had a year-round tan. And he'd always thought her hair, as black as a raven's wing, was beautiful – but not now. She was an Indian! She wasn't his sister!

Rosa saw his flashing eyes and feared something had happened to Jed. 'What is it, Mick? Where is Jed? What's wrong?'

He tried to fight the ugly prejudice in his heart – tried to remind himself that this girl had been brought up with him all his life; that he had known her when they were kids and they'd played in the corral dust together. She'd been his kid sister then. His Rosa. He'd pulled her hair, argued with her, ordered her around. Like Jed and his ma, she had been his family. But now?

Staring, his face a grim mask, he saw her as a Kiowa. The smooth oval face was Indian. She was suddenly a stranger. He knew he just couldn't swallow all the dislike of the Kiowa that had seethed in him the past few years. Shocked, he knew his mind was poisoned and yet there was nothing he could do about it. He just didn't like Indians. For a fleeting second it hit him like a slap in the face that he couldn't think of a single reason why he disliked the Kiowas. He had never been attacked, and it had been a long time since the ranch had suffered at the hands of the Indians. He just hated the tribe because they existed.

Rosa moved quickly to him and placed a hand on his arm. 'Where's Jed? What's happened to him?'

He shrugged her off. 'Nothing's happened to him . . . he's riding along . . .' Sick at heart, he was acutely aware that he didn't want her to touch him.

Rosa exchanged glances with her mother. 'Something is wrong? What is it? Ma, what is wrong?'

'I – I don't know, I'm sure.' Kate Bayner bit her

lip. 'They didn't find the man who came here shouting and yelling last—' She broke off. Her mind was unwilling to pursue that line of thought any further.

Mick couldn't stand the confrontation any longer. He stamped out to the yard and stared unseeingly at the horizon. One thing was clear. Hollister and his hired slaughtermen had not headed straight for the Double O. But maybe they were out there somewhere and maybe they would show up.

He hoped Jed would get back. And soon. Maybe he could face Rosa better with Jed around. There was even a chance he'd get used to the idea of having a Kiowa in the family.

He just wandered around the ranch yard. The sight of Johnny Eagle didn't improve his sour mood. The way the man wore his sixgun, in the scuffed leather holster, like a ranchhand or a white man, was irritating – and yet he knew this was a senseless thought.

Johnny Eagle came up to him, smiling. 'I unsaddled your horse and gave him a good rub-down . . .'

Mick stared at the man. 'What the hell are you smilin' about?'

'Me? It's how I always look.'

'I get the feeling you have secret thoughts.

103

What brought you out here, anyway? Why'd you want to leave Wichita?'

'Just wanted to move on.'

'Being half-Injun, huh? Always on the move, huh?'

'Always, Mr Bayner. All my life I've got only dirty remarks. Just seems they can't look at me and see me as a man. They've got to see a lousy Injun.'

Mick Bayner tightened his lips and looked at the ground as Johnny Eagle went on:

'I can take care of myself. But a woman – she has no defence.'

Mick grated, 'You sure learned how to talk at that mission school.' He glared. 'Why bring up women?'

The reply was delivered smilingly and without insolence. 'I know a Kiowa woman when I see one, my friend.'

Rage flared reply in Mick's brain and his hands whipped up to strike out – but at that moment riders headed for the ranch at a fast pace. There were five men, and one was yelling and singing madly. The other riders had sixguns in their fists. One was astride a big grey; his left arm dangled uselessly, but his big thighs gripped the ribs of his horse and he could ride and shoot with one hand.

'Hollister!' Mick gasped. He began to run for

104

the ranchhouse, shouting to Johnny Eagle, 'Come on! Git to shelter!'

They made it to the cover of the rock and adobe walls even as bullets began to bite at the ground beneath their feet. The hired gunmen were expert shots but they were behaving like drunken cowboys. The shots were flung off without any aim, and the slugs chipped bits from the stone walls of the house. As Mick slammed the door shut and slotted the crossbar, bullets dug into the timber. He turned to Johnny Eagle.

'Get rifles out of the locker. You can earn your keep. These men are killers.'

Mick jumped to the windows in the big living room and threw the shutters into place, then slammed home the bolts. He stared at the narrow slots in the shutters, realizing it was years since they had been used or even thought about. The slots could take a gun, rifle or handgun, and had been fashioned when the house had been built and there was a chance that Indians might be aggressive. If a gun was fired, the glass would be shattered – but that was of little consequence.

Kate Bayner and Rosa were startled. Kate Bayner was speechless, just staring at Mick. It was Rosa, with her quicker reactions, who flung the questions:

'What's happening? Who are those men?'

'They're killers,' muttered Mick. 'Get a gun –
you can handle a gun.'

'Oh, God, where is Jed? Why isn't Jed here?
Why didn't he ride back with you?'

'He wanted to trail these men.'

'You're hiding things from me,' Rosa said.

Mick glared at her. 'There ain't time to start a
whole parcel of explanations. Just get a rifle and
keep down as best you can. These men are bad.'

'What do they want?'

He could have told her that they wanted her
dead and scalped. He turned to his mother. 'Ma,
keep down. We'll deal with these killers!'

Then a flurry of shots came. Slugs sent glass
crashing in the windows. Kate Bayner crouched,
her eyes wide.

Then the shooting subsided and there were
jeering yells from the men outside. One voice
screeched above the others:

'A-yaka a-gumba! Accursed! Accursed! But
revenge is nigh . . . my son – my son.'

Kate Bayner jerked her head around. 'It's him.
He's back – Simon Greer! He's back with his
taunts and his crazy talk. God, I wish I could kill
him.'

Rosa came close to her mother. 'Who is he? That
crazy voice – I remember that. He's the man who
scared me down by the creek.'

Rosa stood up and looked through a slot in the nearest shutter before Mick could stop her. She saw the men riding back and forth, laughing and brandishing handguns. She saw the loco man, the one with the single good eye, and she remembered him. She didn't know any of the others.

Coming back to her mother, she said, 'That's the man who went around the house that night screaming in Kiowa and English ... crazy stuff ... and you said it was the wind. But you knew, didn't you, Ma? You know his name. Simon Greer, you just said.'

Kate Bayner grabbed at the rifle Rosa held and wrestled the gun from the girl. Then she darted to the window and poked the gun out. Within seconds she was firing.

The target was the tall old man who sat upright on his horse and shook his fist at the house. She triggered three shots at him, unthinking. She wanted him dead. All the hate that had built up over the years against Simon Greer's repeated visits to the ranchhouse spurred her on. She was a good shot. True, she hadn't used a gun for some time – and certainly not in anger, but the practice she had had in the harsh years gave her skill. She fired – and missed. Simon Greer's horse reared and she instinctively allowed for this in her next shot. It followed the first within two seconds and

107

tore a hole in the madman's hat. The next shot burned into Simon Greer's face. Even from a distance, Kate Bayner saw the blood wash out his features, and she saw the man topple slowly from the saddle and fall to the ground. She knew he was dead and she exclaimed:

'I've killed him! He's dead! Dead! He'll never bother us again.'

Mick took the rifle from her. She just kept repeating, 'He's dead! Dead! Dead! And I'm glad – glad!'

'Who have you killed, Ma?'

'Simon Greer . . . at last . . . he won't bother us again . . . he won't frighten Rosa . . .'

Cursing, Mick angled a look through the slot in the shutter. He had a framed view of the big man with the useless left arm sitting his horse and staring down at the body. Mick saw only a huddled shape on the ground but he remembered seeing Greer once or twice in Winton and taking no notice of him. All that time he hadn't the slightest idea that this man was tied in with his family. Greer's wild rides around the ranch had come when he'd been busy elsewhere. But now he recalled seeing his mother straining to listen to some queer noises in the night – and he'd attributed it to night-owls. But now, with Jed's explanations flooding his mind, he knew the truth. And his mother had at long last rid herself of this crazy man from her past.

Mick turned back, muttering, 'Damn him! Serves him right for ridin' with that bunch.'

Rosa threw a frightened look at Mick. 'She's killed that awful man?'

'Yes.'

'How terrible. Imagine ... ma ... killing a man.'

Mick retaliated. 'She did it for you.'

'Me?' Rosa held his look. 'What do you mean?'

'Damn it, don't ask me any questions!' He took his rifle and poked it through the shutter slot. 'I think I'll kill one of 'em, too. That Hollister skunk won't be any loss.'

He triggered and was furious when he missed and Hollister went riding off.

Johnny Eagle had a gun poked through the slot in the shutter on the other window. He pumped off some shots without any luck. The sound of drumming hoofs came to them. The men were on the retreat. Johnny Eagle turned to Mick with his familiar smile.

'They've gone. Tell me, who are these men?'

'They're Indian haters,' Mick sneered. 'So you'd best do your damnedest to ward 'em off. They're taking scalps. The one on the big grey is the boss-man.'

'I saw him go. He has only one arm.'

'And a vicious mind. He's mad – like Greer was but in a different way. Don't let the one arm fool you.'

Johnny Eagle said gently, 'You are not Indian. They can't be after your scalp.'

Mick scowled. 'Damn you, mister . . .!'

'If they are Indian haters they are not after you or your brother.'

Clamping his mouth shut, determined not to be led into any more talk, Mick Bayner peered through the slot and waited, wondering about the next move of the killers. He also wondered about Jed. What the devil was keeping him?

It was suddenly silent out on the vast flatland. The gunmen were a long way off, bunched together, apparently conferring. For hired gunslicks, they hadn't planned their attack on the ranchhouse very well; they were the ones without protection and the walls of the house could withstand a siege.

Then came the shout, faint but audible. It was from Hollister. 'You in the house – send that girl out. She's the one we want.'

Rosa's hand went to her mouth. 'Oh, Ma – why, why?'

'Send out that red-hide bitch,' came the savage yell. 'Send her out, I say!'

110

Mick shouted furiously, 'You can go to hell!'

'We've got your brother. Oh, I know all about you and your lousy family. Greer told me plenty and I asked around for the rest . . .'

'Just come in closer and I'll blow your guts to Oklahoma!' shouted Mick. 'Try it, you bastard – just try it! This is my home. No man fires bullets at my home.'

Words came back. 'Seems you didn't hear right, feller. We've got your brother. Send the girl out or he dies. Do you understand?'

For the first time Mick's brain registered the threat clearly. Jed! They had Jed? Was it a trick?

'I don't believe you,' Mick called out desperately.

'We've got him all right. He's strung up by his arms on the only tree for miles around, and we aim to slice his arms to ribbons if we don't get that red-hide bitch.'

The four in the ranchhouse threw glances at each other – frightened glances, guilty, accusing. Kate Bayner had heard everything and was sobbing.

Rosa, wide-eyed with fear, said, 'They want *me*. What do they mean by red hide? That's the way some folks talk about the Indians. Why talk like that about me?'

'It's all just plumb mad talk,' Mick mumbled.

Suddenly she looked terribly Indian to him. He wondered why he had never guessed before. Yet he couldn't throw the truth at her, though savage words trembled on his lips.

'Ma, tell me,' Rosa pleaded. 'Why are they shouting for a red-hide bitch? Tell me. And who was Greer?'

Rosa's gaze searched Kate's face, and when the older woman began to cry piteously, the truth began to penetrate her mind. 'It's me – I'm a red hide! But that's crazy! It's not true. I—'

It was Johnny Eagle who said, 'You're a Kiowa, Rosa. You're a full-blooded Indian, my girl. I know. Don't ask me how – there isn't time to explain.'

Rosa got to her feet and leaned against the wall, her black hair falling across her face, her eyes blazing. All at once her face was a mask of desperate anger. Her figure in the plain cotton dress adopted a lithe, wild attitude. In a flash she looked primitive.

'Kiowa!' she cried. 'Ma, how can that be true? Tell me! You've got to tell me!'

'You're my little girl,' moaned Kate Bayner, her mind refusing to accept reality.

Rosa took a step towards Mick and flung a wild look at him. '*You* know! Tell me what's it all about? *Am* I a red hide? How? Just tell me. Is Johnny Eagle lying? Are those men out there mad?'

112

Mick turned away from her, put an arm against the wall and then leaned his head against his crooked arm. His voice rasped out, 'It's true. You're Kiowa – full blood – like Johnny Eagle says. Ma found you as a child. Greer knew all about you. A man out there called Hollister hates redskins to the point of madness. He just wants to kill you, Rosa – and then scalp you. And if he's got Jed, then God help me. It's you . . . or Jed.'

NINE

Guns Spell Death For One

The lone tree was a natural scaffold. Jed's bound hands had been drawn high above his head by the rope over the branch. His toes barely touched the ground; his horse stood idly by, nosing the grass, the rifle in the scabbard a mockery.

'We could slice him now,' said one man. He had his knife out.

'No,' Hollister had said. 'Leave it. We've got all the time in the world. We get the red bitch, bring her here – and then, boys, we have a real party. Why hurry anything? I want to see this Injun-lover and his mangy so-called sister suffer. Then we take another scalp – a long-haired Kiowa scalp!'

114

There had been laughter at that, particularly from Simon Greer.

They had left him then, riding off with Greer. As the sound of the horses' hoofs had faded in the distance, he'd become aware of the persistent wind. It whistled, prolonged and eerie. He was used to the wind but, strangely, his hearing had tuned to it as if it were something new. It sighed and ran up and down a dreary range of piercing notes. He cursed the depressing sounds and struggled like a madman against the ropes around his wrists.

The only result of his straining had been to rub skin and flesh from his wrists and nearly dislocate his joints. Panting for breath, he knew there was no way of escape. He was alive, sure, but for what purpose? The men were gone. Not a sound came to his ears except the sad wind. They were gone, to get Rosa. Mick and Johnny Eagle would surely put up a fight – unless tricked or taken by surprise – but they were up against hardcase opposition.

For some bitter moments Jed Bayner had wished he had not tangled with Hollister. Maybe, if he had minded his own business, Rosa wouldn't now be in danger.

He had resumed his struggles, cursing and tugging until his skin burst and blood ran down his arms. Only the sky, the scudding clouds and the wind were his company.

When his red rage had subsided, he hung there limply. After an hour his arms were numb, like stumps – like Hollister's arm, he thought.

Then he'd realized that by this time Hollister and his crew would have reached the ranch, but it was beyond his imagination to think of what would happen after that. One thing was sure: they'd kill without compunction.

The sheriff of Winton wasn't noted for reckless-ness, but he still had some sense of duty, and right then it was giving him trouble. He had stood at the office window looking into the quiet street for a long time. He had pounded back and forth across the bare boards of his office, cursing the day he'd taken the job as lawman. At first the job had been easy, ideal for a man whose youthful days were long behind. But now . . .

Art Kortner sighed. Staring out of the window brought no relief from the nagging sense of duty that said he should go out to learn what Downey Hollister and his lawless bunch were doing. He had seen them ride out – but what were they up to? Were they out on another Indian hunt? According to the treaty that said the Kiowas had their own land and legal rights, that was murder.

Killing any man except in a fair fight with witnesses to prove it, was murder – and even that tradition was changing with the times. Pretty soon it would be a crime to kill a man under any conditions, the way new laws had dealt with some gunslingers in towns like Wichita and Tulsa. So what was he going to do about a man like Hollister, right here in his own territory?

Naturally, he wished the army boys would come riding into Winton for a briefing. The sight of three or four would be enough, but he'd had no word concerning his request for action.

Exasperated by his nagging thoughts, Art Kortner finally grabbed at his hat and put it on over his greying, hair. He strapped on his gun and holster, wishing he'd never accepted the badge. Then, rifle in hand, he went to the livery where he kept his horses. He saddled up the wiry brown mustang. Minutes later he rode out. The sun was curving to the west and the biggest part of the day had gone. He had eaten and he could ride around in a wide loop and still be back for a few shots of whisky that night.

He headed west. The trail would take him to the Kiowa Hills, if he had a mind to ride for at least thirty miles, but this was just a patrol. Anyway, he was working . . .

*

They were a desperate group in the sod-roofed ranchhouse. Rosa was pressed against a wall, sheer anger in her body, her eyes filled with defiance. She shot a bitter look at Kate Bayner.

'Why didn't you tell me years ago? And you, Mick. You dislike Indians. I've heard you say it often enough. Well, brother, what now? Do you hate *me*?'

Gripping his rifle hard, Mick sent a flashing look at her. 'Don't give me that, Rosa. Don't you turn on me like that. I've been lied to. Only Jed was told anything, and he kept his trap shut until today. And now we've got a madman out there with hired killers, and—'

'And we're in here hating each other,' she cried.

'That's stupid talk. What the devil can I do if they've got Jed? They'll kill him!'

'Send me out there!' she shrilled. 'Just do as they say. I'm only a Kiowa squaw! Just send me out!'

It was Johnny Eagle who tried to calm them. 'Maybe it's a trick. How do we know they've got him?'

'We know because Jed ain't here,' said Mick. 'Nothing else would have stopped him. And the talk of that tree – I know the place they mean. It all adds up in my mind.'

'Well, what do you reckon to do about it?'

Johnny Eagle asked mockingly. 'Will you ex-change your sister for your brother?'

'She ain't—' Mick bit back the words.

'Yeah, she's just an Indian girl,' Johnny Eagle said. 'Your brother is white. Your choice is plain enough.'

'You can shut your mouth for a start,' Mick said angrily.

Rosa faced Mick defiantly. 'Leave him alone. At least he's not a hypocrite. He's half-Indian and doesn't care who knows it. But look what you've done to me. I'm Indian, it seems, but for years you've brought me up as a Bayner – taught me white habits.' Rosa faced her mother. 'You, Ma, why didn't you tell me? Maybe I could have taken it as a kid; I'd have gotten used to the idea. And that man Greer – he wouldn't have been any menace. But you lived with fear all these years. And now I'm expected to accept that I'm a Kiowa . . .'

Kate Bayner sobbed out, 'You're my little girl . . . you didn't die . . . I didn't bury you . . . Oh Jed, Jed, where are you? Tell them, Jed. Tell them she's my little girl.'

Rosa shook her head in despair, but defiance blazed in her eyes. 'Look at us! Ma is out of her mind! And I'm all Indian. And do you think I care? I think an Indian is as natural as the wind and rain. Johnny Eagle here is beautiful – and he's only half-Kiowa. And you, Mick – you're all twisted up inside, aren't you? Your sister is suddenly someone you hate. Well, I'll show you the result of all the lies!'

She ran into the kitchen. Her furious re-entry to the living room startled Kate Bayner and made Mick curse. Only Johnny Eagle smiled.

For Rosa Bayner had daubed her face with black soot. The marks ran down each cheek and there was one straight line across her forehead. She glared at Mick and then at the woman she had called her mother.

'See? I'm Indian all right. I even feel like an Indian. I realize I've always felt like this – in odd, queer moments – a Kiowa girl!'

'Get that muck off your face!' Mick snarled.

'Why should I? What is my real name? Not Rosa surely? Maybe Little Cloud – or High Sky – and maybe I've got brothers and sisters right up there in the Indian lands.'

Kate moaned. 'Oh, Rosa, my little girl, don't torment me. Clean your face. It's all lies – lies – Greer's lies. But he's dead . . .'

Mick strode over and grasped Rosa's hands. 'You'll get that muck off your face.'

For some moments they wrestled, then Johnny Eagle intervened, his strong arms pulling Mick away from the girl. Mick glared murder at him, and then Rosa began to cry, just like any girl, just like a girl of any race whose nerves had snapped.

As the four in the living room faced each other like antagonists in a tableau, they heard an angry shout from Hollister.

'I'm waiting! Send that red hide out!'

Mick leaped to look through the slot in the shutter. 'Go to hell!'

'Then your brother will die!'

'You think I'm a fool!' raged Mick. 'You're all set to kill him in any case. You wouldn't let Jed go free.'

Silence greeted his statement. Then, 'All right. We'll get you all! We'll burn you out.'

Mick poked his rifle through the slot and waited. He was grimly confident that the house could stand up to any battering – but what of the sod roof? Owing to the dry spell the roof was a thick slab of earth and grass, roots and stems that would burn like peat if a fire took hold. If the roof smouldered and burned, the danger would be smoke. The flat roof was supported by a thin shell of boards.

Mick could see the four riders far out on the plain. They took care to keep at a distance, knowing there were rifles inside the ranchhouse. All at once, as if under instructions, the men rode off.

They went right across the flatland and became mere dots.

'Now is your chance,' said Johnny Eagle. 'Slip out, get to a horse and ride for help.'

Mick looked dubious. 'And leave you?'

'They've got some trick to pull. You'd better decide fast. I can hold them off.'

'Don't *you* want to ride out?' said Mick, his round face suspicious. 'You could get clear away. You don't owe us a thing.'

'Your brother gave me a job and treated me like an equal.'

Mention of Jed made Mick think. 'I might find him. I've got a hunch I know where they've tied him – the tree . . .'

'You'll have to move fast. They're probably lookin' for something to use to burn down this house . . .'

'How the blazes will they get close enough? They've got no cover. They'd be picked off . . .'

'Are you going?' Johnny Eagle demanded. 'Find your brother – then get help if possible.'

'If I find Jed, he'll want to kill Hollister. Never mind any other help.'

'Then slip out to the barn – now! Get a horse.'

'Maybe we could all escape . . .'

'With women? They'd be down on us in minutes.'

Gripping his rifle, Mick Bayner strode to the door. He moved the crossbar and in a second was outside the house. Darting a glance at the far off shapes of men and horses, he ran to the barn and saddled a horse. He pulled the cinch strap tight and then vaulted to the saddle and edged the mount into the open.

Mick shot off on the fresh horse as if spurred on by the devil; taking the opposite direction to that of the four men. He had to get space between him and the four because there were no concealing rocks or hills. He was lucky. Hollister and his crew were a long way off when one of the gunhands spotted the black dot that was the escaping rider.

'That's one of 'em . . .'

'One,' agreed Hollister. 'But the girl is still in the house . . .'

'All right . . . you're the boss.'

Johnny Eagle barred the door again and turned to Rosa with a smile. 'He's away. If they attack, I'll kill some of them. They might sicken of this mad business if a couple of them die.'

She had composed herself again, leaning against the wall, the rifle resting butt-end on the floor. She looked bitterly at Kate Bayner, realising the terrible differences between them. Somehow it was now glaringly obvious that they were not mother and daughter. A great secret had been revealed which had blasted them apart. And yet this frightened woman had cared for her all her life. The bond was not entirely broken.

Johnny Eagle came close to Rosa and with a bandanna began to wipe the soot marks from her face. 'You are not a warrior – and you are not a squaw. You are like me, something different.'

Close to him, she sensed the affinity between them. His shirt was open and his tanned chest reminded her that her own body was not pale and white. All these years! She should have guessed. Now, staring at Johnny Eagle, she was aware of complex emotions. He was like herself!

'Those men will be back,' murmured Johnny Eagle, 'so I'd like to talk quick to you, Rosa. If you will let me, I will care for you . . .'

She saw the deep sincerity in his dark eyes and turned away, confused. 'This is some sort of madness . . . I – I have to think. There is Jed . . .' She broke off, wondering why a vision of Jed Bayner seemed to be before her, smiling, watching her.

'He is white,' said Johnny Eagle. 'How can he be for you? Has he spoken to you?'

'No.'

'You are Kiowa and I am half-blood. We understand each other . . .'

'But . . . Jed . . .'

124

'Surely he has looked upon you only as a sister? He can't change now. Anyway, I want you for my woman.' A rough edge had crept into his voice. He took hold of her shoulders and she trembled. But two things were happening: Kate Bayner was watching them with anger etched in her face. No Kiowa or 'breed would dare hold her Rosa!

Grimly, she lifted her rifle.

But shouts came from outside the ranchhouse and some bullets thudded into the stout window shutters.

Johnny Eagle pulled Rosa down to the floor. They crouched and stared into each other's eyes. She had been told she was Kiowa, suddenly and savagely. Her brother had turned against her, and all at once her mother seemed strange and distant. But Johnny Eagle was her kind. She could seek sympathy from him. At that moment even Jed was a stranger. Johnny Eagle was there, handsome and strong.

Then came Hollister's shout:

'You in there – send that bitch out. We can use slings to set fire to that roof. We don't have to come too close . . .'

A volley of shots was thrown at the house. The gunhands were using their rifles. The windows were the target and the remaining fragments of glass fell with a tinkling sound.

Kate Bayner could stand the terror no longer. She leaped to a window shutter, poked her rifle out. She was oblivious of danger.

Before Rosa or Johnny Eagle could pull her away from the window shutter, another volley hit the house. Dull thudding sounds came as the shutters took some of the slugs. A stray bullet whined through a slot. Johnny Eagle and Rosa instinctively ducked. But the bullet took Kate Bayner in the forehead.

She fell back, twisting, facing the other two. The gun fell to the floor. Her eyes went dead. She fell as Rosa jumped to her side.

If Johnny Eagle felt any compassion, he didn't allow it to show. Dark eyes implacable, he said, 'She's dead. We've got to get out of here, Rosa, you and I.'

But he wondered if he had left it too late. Mick had seized a chance but now the house was surrounded and pretty soon they would start to fire the roof.

TEN
Rosa Decides

They were sitting their horses, knees tight against the ribcages, boots hard on the stirrups and rifles at the ready. They had sent volleys of shots at the ranchhouse and hadn't had a single bullet in reply. And so they ceased shooting and looked expectantly at Downey Hollister. His mouth was an angry slit and his rifle was tucked under his one good arm.

'All right,' Hollister said, 'we'll get a little closer. Ralph, you ready with your sling? Do you think you can lob a burning brand onto that roof?'

'Sure,' said the man with the sardonic face and the lean figure of a starving rat. 'I'm pretty good at this.'

They had collected a heap of dried roots and

127

tinder and Hollister had used a flask of brandy on one torch. It was ready to light.

'Damn well defying me!' mumbled Hollister, his eyes glittering. 'I wonder just who is in there – apart from that red-hide bitch.'

'One got away,' said Ralph.

'I figure that was the other Bayner brother,' said Hollister. 'He don't matter. I'll cripple the other one, then kill him.'

'Should I start lighting a brand?' asked the man.

'Sure, fire it, you fool! Do you always need orders?'

Ralph bridled. 'Don't bawl me out, Mr Hollister. You like to kick orders around. You act like you're God when you feel that way.'

'Get busy with that damned sling, man!'

Ralph exchanged looks with his two partners. The young fellow who sported two guns, grinned and winked. A lot younger than Hollister, and certainly not sharing his mania, they secretly felt contempt for the man who paid them. In their view he was just an aging maniac who had plenty of cash.

'Maybe we can git that red-hide bitch out with a whole skin,' chuckled the young two-gun thug.

'You got her body on your mind?' jeered the third man.

128

'Why not? A squaw brought up as a white . . . that could be interestin'.'

Hollister glared at them, leaning forward in his saddle. 'I'll be the one to say what happens to her.'

'You just want her dead, don't you?'

'I want her out of that house first,' Hollister said, 'and then we'll take her to where we've got Bayner. Jed Bayner will die slowly, along with the bitch . . .'

The third gunhand had been scanning the horizon. He had keen eyesight and had seen the dust.

'We've got company,' he snapped. 'Over there – to the west.'

The others froze, staring, the ranchhouse temporarily forgotten.

It was Ralph who muttered, 'That's a helluva lot of horses.'

'White men?' asked Hollister.

Ralph stared hard. The dust hid the riders who came on at a reckless pace. Then he said, 'Indians!'

'Kiowa?' spat Hollister. 'How many?'

'Too damned many for my comfort,' yelled the other.

'You've got the eyesight . . . how many?'

'I tell you – one hell of a bunch . . .'

'Out here? Away from the reservation?'

Ralph suddenly cried out, 'Must be about fifty.'

'Fifty?' the other gunhand gasped. 'Hell, let's get! We can't take them on!'

Hollister nudged his horse around without holding the reins. He raised his rifle with his good arm. 'We could take some of them,' he said, and his eyes took on a crazy glitter.

'Act your age!' screamed Ralph. Fear was chilling his guts. 'They'll do for us in the end.' He turned to the others. 'Kit – Mac – let's ride!'

Hollister attempted to argue with them, apparently blind to the approaching danger. He wheeled his horse as the other three jigged their mounts around in confusion. He shouted, 'We can take some of them dirty red hides! We can take 'em and ride out. Stick with me, men . . . it's a chance to cut down these stinkin' coyotes – rid the land of 'em!'

'You're loco!' screamed Ralph. 'Maybe they're after us.'

'Must be the reason,' agreed the young two-gun called Kit.

'Damn you, you rebellious scum!' howled Downey Hollister. 'I want 'em all dead! I'm paying you. Stick with me!'

But the three men had assessed the danger a lot better than the Indian-hater and were already pushing their mounts into a fast lope.

Hollister spurred his big grey around fuming

with rage. He sent bitter glances back at the
large party of Indians, and then he, too, was
racing off.

In the ranchhouse Johnny Eagle and Rosa
watched the hurried departure of the killers and
wondered why the attempt to burn the house
hadn't been carried out. When Hollister and his
men had disappeared, Johnny Eagle slipped out
of the house and looked around for the reason. He
spotted a large group of fast-ridden Indian ponies,
an unusual sight these peaceful days. He watched
them for some minutes and was about to return to
the house when Rosa joined him.

'That's the reason why they left,' he said.
'They're scared. And judging from what Mick told
us, I don't blame them. Kiowas.'

'It's a large party. I've never seen so many.' She
stared into the distance at the riders. Unless they
veered off they would pass the ranchhouse by a
good two miles. 'They could be in trouble for leaving the reservation,' she added.

'If the army was anywhere near to check on
them,' agreed Johnny Eagle. He took her arm.
'Come on – we've got to leave here, now.'

Walking back to the sturdy house that had been
her home all her life, she said vaguely, 'Leave?'

'Those killers might return.'

'But the Kiowas are chasing them . . .'

'I figure they'll give them the miss,' he said grimly. 'They've got big horses and unless one takes a tumble or breaks a leg, they'll carry those men right back to Winton. The Kiowas will turn off long before they reach the town. They don't want trouble with the army or the Indian agent and maybe further restrictions for breaking the treaty. They've got good hill land and it suits them. But I think we ought to leave in case those killers ride back. They might, in the darkness.'

'But Jed and Mick will be back by then,' she cried.

'Mick hates you. You're a Kiowa, remember . . .'

She nodded. 'But, Jed—'

'Mick has yet to find him.'

'I – I hope he's all right.'

'He's a white man and not for you,' he told her.

'I always thought of him as my big brother, yet there were times when he was more than that . . . times when I felt so strangely close to him, and it upset me because I was his sister . . .'

He led her into the house. 'We must gather some things together – guns, food, blankets. I'll get the horses ready. We've got to leave, Rosa.'

When he was outside, seeing to two horses, she looked down at her mother's body lying in a pathetic huddle and felt terribly alone. She looked at Kate Bayner for a long time, recalling the good times, the days when they were a happy family. She saw mental pictures of Jed at roundup time, coming into the house bone-tired and dirty, smelling of hide and sweat and dust; her mother in the kitchen – always the kitchen – cooking and cleaning and washing. Life at the ranch had been hard and frugal, but she had known nothing else. And now it was gone, along with the woman she'd known as her mother. Kate Bayner had kept a secret from her all these years; the secret of her birth and origin. Later, Jed had known – and he'd said nothing to her. What had been Jed's real thoughts? She remembered the night on the porch when she had kissed him – and then shrank back in confusion because she knew him as her brother. What had he said? Yes . . . he would look after her.

But what did he mean? Did he intend to look after her as his sister? Did that mean he'd have gone on deceiving her?

Suddenly the whole house, now so silent and strange, was a place from which she wanted to run. She turned and caught sight of herself in a mirror. She saw the copper-hued skin that she had always thought was just a deep tan; she saw her long black hair – Indian hair. And her eyes were liquid and brown – certainly not like those of Mick and Jed. How could she have thought she

133

was their sister?

With a kind of choking cry she turned and ran from the house and almost into Johnny Eagle's arms. He was leading two horses. He stopped her and held her with one arm, smiling, comforting. 'Hey, this is no time for tears.'

She looked up. 'Isn't it? My life has suddenly changed. Oh, you're right, Johnny. I've got to get away from this place.'

'And from Jed?' he said roughly.

'Yes – from Jed. I've just looked at myself in the mirror. I'm a Kiowa all right. And Jed is white. He doesn't want me.' She looked at him. 'Not the way you do—'

Minutes later they were ready. He tied saddle-bags to the horses, water canteens and bedrolls. He put a rifle in each scabbard and wore his steeple-shaped hat with the snakeskin band. Rosa did not need a hat; she tied her hair back with a wide ribbon, in a pony-tail down her back. Then she slipped a shawl around her shoulders and got into the saddle, her dress hemline falling naturally around her legs.

Johnny Eagle eyed her appreciatively. She was all woman and he would take her as his wife as soon as they could reach a mission where the ceremony could be performed. Now that his mind was made up, nothing or no one would stop him.

They rode away from the house, passing the body of Simon Greer, sprawled out and looking so slight, so small.

Many miles away across the monotonous land that had no hills, Mick Bayner pushed his horse to its limit. He had no trouble finding the spot where there was only the one tree for miles around. He'd been this way many times. And he could see the sycamore from a long way off. As he got closer he saw his brother. He kicked his horse, urging it to go even faster.

When he finally reached the tree, Mick leaped from the saddle, hauled out his working knife from the sheath in his belt and slashed at the hemp. He was barely able to hold Jed's weight in his arms. His brother was heavy. Mick lowered him to the ground and began slapping his face.

Jed's horse stood close by, nibbling at grass. Mick ran to the animal, got the water canteen from the saddlehorn and uncorked it. He returned to Jed and dribbled some liquid into his mouth. Then he cut the lengths of rope and massaged his brother's wrists. Finally Jed opened his eyes. He stared at Mick.

'Help me up . . .'

'Take it easy. Sip some water – your lips are swollen. You can't ride yet. How'd they surprise

135

you?'

'A little trick with three dead Indians . . .' Jed choked out the details between sips of water. 'And you? How the blazes did you know where to find me?'

Mick began to tell him about the attack. Jed levered himself to his feet. 'You left them?'

'They'll be all right. The house can stand anything short of a cannon.'

'Maybe, but we can't be sure.'

'They've got rifles and that 'breed you hired seems willing to fight.'

'Does that surprise you, Mick?'

Mick ignored the question and went on: 'Ma killed that Greer *hombre*. Shot him dead.'

Jed swallowed. 'And . . . Rosa?'

'Rosa knows she's a Kiowa.'

'You told her? Why?'

Jed Bayner straightened and towered over his brother.

'I had to tell her. It all came out. Hollister was shouting all kinds of filthy things. And that 'breed finished it by telling Rosa to her face that she was a full-blooded Kiowa. That bastard knew all along.'

'He knew?'

'Sure,' said Mick bitterly. 'And I don't trust him.'

'You've left Ma and Rosa . . .'

'I mean I don't trust him with our adopted

Kiowa sister,' Mick ground out. There was a sneer in his voice. 'I think we'd better get back home if you can hang onto that horse.'

'We're going back sure enough,' gritted Jed Bayner. 'I want Hollister and his outfit. I'll kill that swine.'

He had to be helped up into his saddle. His arms were still numb. He could not make a fist or even move his fingers.

They moved off. Jed had the reins wrapped around one hand. His other arm swung loosely but with every passing minute the numbness lessened. Soon he was able to make a fist.

Mick's horse was loath to reach a full lope after the hard ride. They went across the flatland at an easy gallop.

They were about halfway to the ranch when they spotted the lone rider. As Mick and Jed shortened the gap between them and the rider they discovered his identity.

'The sheriff of Winton,' snapped Mick. 'The man who doesn't want to know. What's he doin' out here?'

'Damned if I know. But we'll cross his trail and you can holler to him. We're not wastin' any time.'

Art Kortner saw them and came to meet them, so there was only a minimum of delay. As Jed and Mick wouldn't stop the onward rush of their mounts, he rode along with them.

'Hey . . . you two – seen any sign of that Hollister cuss?'

'Do you figure to arrest him, badgeman?' This from Mick.

Kortner puffed out his cheeks. 'I might – if I had a stack of evidence and some help. But four gunnies is too much for one man.'

'Well, listen to this, Kortner,' said Jed. 'They killed and scalped three more Kiowas just five miles from here. And right now they're attacking our ranchhouse. They figure to kill Rosa and anybody else who gets in their way. So are you riding with us – or are you heading back for your evening tot?'

Art Kortner gulped. The badge on his vest was beginning to feel like a millstone. 'I'll ride with you, fellers, sure thing.'

With the sheriff at their side, they pressed on. Grass and stones flew from under flying hoofs. The shades of night were beginning to fail. The wind, as always, was whining. With full darkness the wind would take over and blow mournfully through the night. There was always the chance it might build into a twister, tearing up all before it except the stoutest construction.

The three men rode at a fast pace when they came into sight of the ranchhouse. They wondered at the silence. Mick didn't understand. He had expected to run into a fight.

Then they saw the black mess that was the roof. Part of it had caved in. Smoke still curled up.

Mick didn't know that Hollister had fled with his men but had then returned and, filled with satanic anger, had fired the house.

ELEVEN
'I Want You!'

When Rosa and Johnny Eagle made camp there was a quarter moon and stars sprinkled the sky. They were at the start of the undulating coulees that marked the beginning of the Kiowa Hills – reservation land. He built a fire and it glowed cheerfully, keeping the shadows back. They ate a meal of bacon and fried bread and now each had a tin mug of coffee.

'We can marry at the mission near the Indian agent's office,' said Johnny Eagle. 'That's a real official wedding – or it can be a Kiowa celebration.'

Rosa was silent. She stared unseeingly at the fire as he continued:

'I can approach Chief White Horse – or Tsen-T'ainte, as he is known in the Kiowa tongue. I know him.'

140

Red Hide

'So you've been this way before?' Rosa said.

'My father brought me here a number of times. He was Kiowa – my mother was white. I leave it to you, Rosa. We can live as white-eyes or return to the Indian ways.'

'I have been brought up as white,' she said. 'You know that. You know I'm white in everything but the colour of my skin and the texture of my hair.'

'You have lovely hair. You're really a beautiful girl.'

She smiled for the first time since darkness had fallen. 'You sound like any other man handing out a compliment to a girl. I – I don't think you're really Indian, Johnny Eagle.'

'I'm not. But, as I told you, Rosa, you can choose the way you want to live.'

'And the man I want to live with?' The question bubbled out before she realised the gravity of it. 'I mean . . . what if I don't love you, Johnny Eagle?'

He set down his tin mug. 'You will. We're meant for each other. What else but fate could have put two like us together?'

She was beginning to feel unsure again. Perhaps the dark shadows beyond the fire built up her sense of insecurity, or maybe it was just feminine foolishness. She wondered why she was running away. Was she running because she was Indian – and Jed and Mick were white and not

141

really her brothers? Was she running because Mick hated the Kiowas and she thought Jed had lied to her? And Johnny Eagle was here, helping her to run. And somewhere in the night, Hollister fed his hate.

'We shouldn't be here together,' she muttered at last. 'It isn't right.'

'I want you, Rosa.' With sudden purpose, he moved closer to her. He took her in his arms. 'I mean now . . .'

'No!'

'Hasn't there ever been a man?'

She stared into his face. He was handsome and there was power in his body; he was the kind who could master a girl. She shivered a little, feeling his masculinity. She said, 'There hasn't been a man . . . not like that . . .'

'Then it's time. I love you, Rosa . . .'

His grip on her shoulders was no longer tender. Then his hand slid down to touch a breast. She hesitated for a moment, allowing the caress, then she twisted away from him. 'No . . . please, Johnny. When I marry you – if I marry you . . .'

'There is no *if*.' He held her again and his mouth sought her lips. He kissed her with a rough tenderness. But it was the resumption of his caress that made Rosa start back like a wild animal and cry out. 'Please, Johnny . . . we're not sure of each other. It – it's madness. Why can't we just talk?'

'Can talk show you how much I want you?'

'Maybe . . . oh, Johnny, I'm so mixed up I could cry. I do like you . . . sure . . . and maybe I'll marry you. Can't we just sleep and see what tomorrow brings?'

He reached out and gripped her again. 'We'll sleep, Rosa – together.'

He made a big mistake. With the strength of the young, she fought clear of his hands and jumped to her feet. In the warm red glow of the fire, with the simple dress swishing around her limbs, she made a desirable picture, but at that moment she was shocked and dismayed at the way Johnny Eagle was treating her. He was too abrupt. Maybe, if he had wooed her, she might have succumbed . . .

His next mistake was in trying to grab at her as she stood looking down at him. She lithely avoided his hands. Then, as he jumped up, his anger evident, she turned and ran.

She sprinted through the darkness, wildly, without any idea of where to go. The glow of the fire was suddenly a long way behind her. Looking back, she nearly fell to the ground. He was yelling after her, furious commands for her to come back. She didn't; she plunged on and then sank down in a hollow, frightened. There was no place she could run to. She crouched down and eventually he found her.

Breathing heavily, he sank down beside her. Shaking his head, expressing his own doubts, he said gently, 'Sweet Rosa, I won't hurt you. I won't touch you again . . . unless you let me. Come back to the fire. You can't stay here. Tomorrow will be another day for both of us. We can figure it out then . . .'

Hollister looked sarcastically at his men. Dawn was streaking over the land. The wind was still whining mournfully across the grass and juniper-filled coulees, but it would die down as the day warmed. Ralph was looking sour, trying to get a fire going from bits of dried roots and a few twigs he'd gathered from the brush. The men were in a complaining mood. He knew what was wrong with them; they were jittery after seeing the Kiowas in full force. For a long time the hunting of Indians had been conducted as a gun-game, with the redman always the surprised party and usually only in twos or threes. It had been like hunting bear in the hills.

'All right,' said Hollister, 'there's only one thing I want – that sneaking red-hide bitch. I want her dead. She's got no right to live. I say the redskin

144

has to be rubbed out altogether. That's the answer to the problem – get rid of 'em. Then there'll be no trouble – no dirty villages and squaws with lousy papooses – just us whites.' Downey Hollister began to rub his withered arm, his eyes glinting sickly.

'You don't even know what she looks like,' said Ralph.

'An Injun girl in white woman's clothes, that's what,' said Hollister.

'Well, she got clean away —'

'We got the old woman,' stated Hollister. 'She was the one who brought up that bitch – so we fixed her.'

'But lost Jed Bayner,' sneered Ralph. 'Gone – ropes cut . . .'

'Obviously his brother got to him.' Hollister tried to lift his dead arm. He frequently tried to move the arm – when he was unwilling to accept a chunk of semi-dead flesh. 'It's a wonder we didn't cross paths, but we didn't. Anyway, we sure fired that damned ranchhouse.'

'Yeah. And we rode a helluva lot of mangy country to get away from those savages and loop back. For what – to burn the roof of an empty house!'

'I thought the girl might be there.'

'Well, she sure wasn't. She lit out – and now we're headin' for Kiowa country because you got a hunch.'

'What the hell's eating you, Ralph?' Downey
Hollister shouted in a rage. 'You scared of Injuns?
You want more money?'

'I'd sooner be in a saloon than out here,' said
Ralph.

'You need money to drink,' sneered Hollister.

Ralph looked around and sighed. 'This place . . .
Kiowa Hills ahead of us . . . that miserable flatland behind us – and all because of one Injun girl.
Hell, why not just run down a few Indians somewhere else – somewhere safe – like we been doin'?
Shoot their stinking guts out and then take their
scalps, though we got more of them than we can
handle. I'm sick of toting a bag of stinking hair!'

'There was a time when we got bounty money
for 'em!' Hollister raged at his rebellious hireling.

'You're crazy. Them scalps will have us hangin'
from a tree – that's if the Kiowas don't get us first.
Bounty! Hell! Don't you know what year this is?
I've heard it said there won't ever be another
Indian war. We got treaties and telegraphs and
railroads. And the Indians have rights . . .'

'You're a loose-mouthed bastard!' Hollister
crouched and his right hand touched the butt of
his Colt.

Ralph tried to laugh the tension away. 'I sure
am loose-mouthed. And I'm sayin' it so's Mac and

Kit can hear. I don't like this notion of heading for the Kiowa Hills just because you got a hunch the girl cut this way.'

Mac, the other lean gunny, nodded. 'That's right. Who says she'd head this way?'

'She's Kiowa.'

'She was brought up white. Least, we're goin' by what we were told by that loco old man, Greer. Glad he's dead. His screechin' was gittin' on my nerves.'

'Look, she ran out – got a horse. I say she'd head up here. Why? Because she's a squaw at heart.'

'Hell, she could be in Winton.' Ralph's disgust was in the open. He was testifying that he had lost confidence in Hollister.

'I say she's headed this way,' Hollister all but screamed in reply. His obsession was taking his nerves to a razor-edge. And his madness was slowly consuming him. Ralph knew it. And Kit, the two-gun youth, had a permanent sneer for Hollister these past two days. Mac was getting doubtful, too.

'There were fifty Injuns in that bunch that chased us,' said Ralph.

'An exaggeration. Maybe thirty. We don't know. Anyway, if you all quit arguing, we'll cut sign of that girl long short of the Indian villages.'

They finished their breakfast, mixing obscenities with complaints that they were sick of beans and bacon, and then they climbed into their saddles and nosed their horses out. They went on in silence, bitter men who had tolerated each other's company for too long.

Although their dirty, unshaven faces were lined with caution and they kept a good lookout, they were soon among hills and rolling gullies that could hide a house. Trees began to appear on grassy slopes. There were springs bubbling into rocky basins. It was a land that fed wild life. It was also the habitat of the Kiowa, although they had been pushed back from the plains in the days when the buffalo had been plentiful.

They knew they were riding into danger but they figured it would be Indian. They were taken by surprise when they rounded a hillock of grass and rock and saw three men riding towards them.

'Bayner, by thunder!' yelled Hollister and he grabbed at his handgun.

But rifles spoke first, for Jed, Mick and Kortner had their Winchesters cradled in their arms. The bullets sang wickedly around Hollister and his crew and one slug found flesh.

It was the lean gunny called Mac, who yelled in agony and fell flat against his horse's neck, dropping his Colt. He rolled from the saddle. Hollister and the other two dived for cover.

TWELVE

Death Sorts It Out

Hollister and his two men sent careful glances down to the floor of the grassy gully where Mac writhed and clawed inch by inch towards them. Hollister and his two sidekicks had found shelter behind a mound of earth that had a bush growing out of the topsoil. The horses had scampered away with kicking heels the moment the men had dived for cover. Down the shallow valley the two Bayners and the sheriff had worked their horses behind a slab of rock that rose like a monument from the bunch grass. They were perfectly safe – so long as they stayed there.

They'd have to shoot it out. One group could, of course, decide to retreat. In the meantime, Mac crawled and screamed in agony. He'd move a yard or so and collapse, curling up. Then, moaning and with blood dripping from him, he would try to claw his way forward a little more. He could barely see his friends. He howled to them:

'Help me . . . gimme a hand . . . Ralph, Kit . . . gimme a hand . . .'

Ralph snarled at the wounded man. No partner was worth dying for. Any man who dashed across that bare space would be cut down.

Hollister was making sucking sounds with his breathing and, poking his handgun around the hillock, followed the gun with his eyes just enough to get a view of the big rock. He cursed his bad luck. Jed Bayner was the biggest blot on his life. Bayner and that miserable Kiowa bitch. If only he would wipe them out.

Kit had hefted his twin guns and was snaking forward on his belly with the idea of getting a glimpse of a target, but he exposed only inches of his head and he was fast enough to jerk back when three slugs bit into the earth near him.

Behind the big slab of rock, Jed Bayner glanced at his brother. 'We got one of them.'

'Evens it up a bit,' Mick grunted. 'Seems you were right in thinking Kiowa country would give a lead – but you were thinkin' of finding Rosa here. We ain't cut sign of her or that 'breed.'

'I was sure they'd head up here because I know

Johnny Eagle has been this way before.'

'He told you that?'

'He said he came into the hills as a kid.'

'Seems like Hollister got the same hunch.' Mick's round face, stubbled with beard, twisted bitterly. 'I'm gonna kill that skunk. He shot ma . . .'

They went silent. Kortner hunched against the rock, his gun in a sweating hand. He wondered why he had allowed himself to be talked into this play. Winton seemed a long way off.

'All right,' muttered Jed, 'let's give 'em hell!'

He and Mick poked out the rifles and took aim, waiting for the slightest movement behind the hillock. The targets were there, imperceptible, holding only long enough for a shot to be fired off, but Jed and Mick had the advantage of rifle power. The other men had only handguns – their long guns were still in the saddle holsters and the horses had spooked.

Jed and Mick pumped off some shots that were near misses. Slugs came their way, too, because the three hardcases had plenty of gun-skill. It was a case of a man lingering too long over a shot; then he'd take a slug, maybe between the eyes.

The man called Mac was still writhing on the grass. He was crying out for help and his heart was pumping blood through the gaping wound in

151

his stomach. There was a red trail over the grass. Jed was sick of listening to him. For all he knew this man might be the one who killed his mother.

Jed took aim at the dying man and triggered. The shot dug into the body and made it jerk. It was the last convulsion. The moaning ceased.

Jed snapped to Mick, 'I'm gonna work around 'em. I don't figure to cower here all day.'

'They're gunslicks.'

'To hell with that.' Jed turned to the sheriff. 'Kortner, earn your blamed keep. Help Mick keep me covered. I'm goin' around them – before they figure to do the same with us. You let me down, Kortner, and I'll make you eat that badge.'

Jed crept out, flat as a snake, his rifle sliding over the grass. He could maybe circle the gunmen – if Mick and Kortner could keep them pinned down.

To give the lawman his due, his gun began to thunder the moment Jed left the cover of the slab of rock. The slugs did their work. Hollister and his two men hugged the ground. Mick watched Jed's progress. When Jed reached a boulder and sank down, Mick nudged Kortner and both men began reloading their guns. Then they took the challenge to the hardcases again, flinging shots at the hillock while Jed ran for higher ground. Even Art Kortner began to lose his fear, although sweat streaked his grey sidewhiskers.

The killers' horses ran further off. The three mounts belonging to Jed's party were safe, having been hitched. Hollister sensed what was going on. He threw frantic glances around the terrain for sign that his hunch was right. He spotted Jed high above them, just about behind them, and with a snarl he flung off two shots.

But Jed was too far off for a handgun to reach him with accuracy. He settled behind the rock he had picked out. The cards were all his. He had a rifle and he could take his time. But that didn't mean he'd waste time. He wouldn't give Hollister and his men a chance to work to new cover.

Jed aimed and triggered. He had sighted his rifle on the tall, lean gunhand. The man was twisted around, caught in a terrible moment of indecision. He had seen Jed high above him. With a shout of fear, he tried to run, a dive that might have gained him a new hideout.

Jed's bullet took him between the shoulderblades and tore a hole in the man's heart. Ralph seemed to dive forward under the impact, but when he hit the ground he lay still.

Jed sighted on the young two-gun braggart. The matching Colts were not of much use to him at that moment and certainly not in the eternity to which he was heading. The gunman had got warnings from Ralph's bolt for freedom and he was scuttling on all fours, his guns momentarily pointed anywhere but at a target.

Jed aimed and fired as if the man represented fleeing carrion. He saw the lean figure roll over and over. Jed thought he had hit him, but he wasn't sure until the killer finally quit bouncing like a bundle of old rags and lay still.

In a second of flashing thought, Jed realized he should have taken Hollister first. But no matter. Hollister was trapped.

But there was animal cunning working in Downey Hollister's frantic brain. He had dived to a new boulder. His good hand was white and bloodless and his fingers gripped the gunbutt. He lay still, huddled, his mind working.

Jed waited. If he didn't get a look at Hollister, then Mick or even Kortner might get a chance. So he waited, his guts filled with satisfaction. Death was there to be handed out. He'd wait – and he'd think of his mother while he waited.

The shooting stopped. Then slowly, Hollister's last remnants of sanity slipped. He couldn't believe he was alone; he'd hired men to do his filthy work for so long he couldn't realize they had ceased to exist. 'Ralph . . . Kit . . . what the hell . . . get them . . . get them!' Yet he could see they were dead.

Jed Bayner decided to finish it. He shouted,

'Give up, Hollister. You can throw that gun away. Let me see it go high and wide. Then you come out with your good hand in the air.'

'Go to hell!'

'Then die!'

Hollister's face worked convulsively. 'You can't do this to me. I'm Downey Hollister. I could buy you up, lock, stock and barrel. Tell you what, Bayner . . . you let me go and I'll give you all the money you'll ever want. I've got money – plenty – I struck it lucky with gold years ago before them damned Indians crippled me. What do you say?'

Mick's harsh yell came from the tall rock. 'You killed ma, you slimy snake!'

Jed added, 'Come out!'

Unexpectedly, the man obeyed. He moved swiftly for a man of his age. He came walking out from behind the boulder. The gun dangled from his hand which was held high.

'Drop the gun!' snapped Jed as he walked slowly to the man. He saw the fear in Hollister's glittering eyes. Then the gun dropped. Hollister approached slowly.

'You'll die, Hollister,' Jed told him. 'You and your men killed my mother. You've murdered scores of Indians. You'll hang!'

'Like hell!' said Hollister.

He was only a few yards from Jed, glaring at

him with his terrible eyes, his good arm still high. Then he leaped and the arm flashed down. With the speed that only madness and panic can bring to a desperate man, his hand whipped to the knife in his belt sheath. Then the knife was out, glinting in the sun. He was almost on Jed when the rifle went off.

Jed triggered his shot into the man's big chest at point-blank range and then jumped back. Only momentum kept Hollister moving. Then his legs buckled and his big body crumpled. The knife fell.

The body at his feet, Jed felt a savage impulse to fill it full of lead. But that wouldn't bring back his mother. This dirty specimen with the itch to kill had snapped out the life of a wonderful woman. Jed turned away, blindly, not aware that Mick and Art Kortner were there, staring down at the body.

'Well, that does it,' muttered Kortner. 'We've sure got some bodies to tote back to town. Well, I can testify it was a fair fight . . .'

'You do that, Kortner,' said Jed Bayner. 'You testify your damn head off. And you can tote the bodies back yourself. I've got other things to do.'

He wanted to find Rosa; he wanted to talk to her about many, many things. He wanted to know why she had run off, why had she not waited somewhere near the ranch-house after Hollister and his men had gone. Why hadn't she waited for them to return?

Jed and his brother parted company with Kortner, despite the man's protests that he needed help to round up the horses and sling the bodies over the saddles.

They rode deeper into Kiowa country.

It was past midday when they found Rosa and Johnny Eagle outside the Indian agent's office. Ahead was an Indian village of wigwams, covered in bark, matting and hides. Women and children were everywhere, and cook-pots were slung over embers. The office was set against a redstone bluff, some way from the village, and Jed and Mick's arrival created little interest.

Jed had eyes only for Rosa. He started forward the moment he got down from his horse. 'Rosa . . . it's all over. Hollister is dead. I've come for you . . . you've got nothing to fear.'

It was Johnny Eagle who stopped him from taking the girl's arm. 'I aim to marry her, Bayner.'

Jed towered above him. 'Is that why you ran off?'

'We've talked of marriage . . .' Johnny Eagle stood close to the girl. His gun lay snug in its holster, his hat was pushed back to reveal his dark hair.

Mick went into a rage. 'Why, you rotten twister,

is that how you repay us? It figures for a half-Indian—'

'Rosa is wholly Kiowa,' retorted the half-breed.

'Damn you, I know that!' Mick looked at the silent girl. Now he saw only the girl he'd known all his life; a great kid who'd laughed and joked with him. They had shared the same table and argued. He knew exactly what she liked . . . the way she grinned . . . her sense of humour . . . and in that flash of intuition he knew that whatever Rosa was racially, she was his sister.

'Rosa,' he said pleadingly, 'I don't have any bad ideas of who you are or what you are. But I guess the choice is yours. You can marry Johnny Eagle – if that's what you want. I just want you to know.'

Now Jed and Rosa stared at each other, each seeking truth in the other's eyes. For a long time after Mick had spluttered into silence they looked searchingly at each other, then Jed held out his hands. He said simply, 'What is it to be, Rosa? Only you know the answer. I can tell you right here and now that you mean the world to me – and I don't think of you as my sister.'

She spoke. 'I'm a red-hide . . .'

'That's the last time you'll speak like that,' said Jed. 'I told you long ago I wanted to take care of you – protect you . . . as a wife.'

Sudden anger leaped into Johnny Eagle's

heart. He jumped forward, in front of Rosa, confronting Jed Bayner, and his gun flashed into his hand. 'Why should you take her from me? I could kill you right now . . .'

Rosa suddenly moved. She walked deliberately to Jed's side and faced Johnny Eagle. She clung to Jed's arm. She said gently, 'Put that gun away, Johnny. You won't use it. I – I guess I've always loved Jed. I shouldn't have encouraged you, Johnny. Can you forgive me?'

The gun slowly angled down. Johnny Eagle seemed to lose his anger as swiftly as it had come. He holstered the gun.

'I guess it has to be. I'm the loser.' He attempted a smile. 'Good luck, Bayner. You'll take care of her, I know. I figure most of the troubles are behind you – if Hollister is dead.'

'And you?' Jed asked. 'What are you going to do?'

'Ride on. There's always another land over the next hill . . .' He turned and whispered, 'Goodbye, Rosa . . .'

It was later, when they were alone, that Jed kissed her. The old image of brother and sister dissolved and would never return. They both knew they were destined to be man and wife.

'We're going home,' Jed said. 'There's a church in Winton – and they ain't had a wedding for months. I aim to promise to love and cherish you, Rosa.'

'And I'll do that, too,' she laughed.

'There's one more thing,' said Jed with a grin. 'We sure need a new roof on the house – and it won't be sod. We'll put a real roof on – just you see, my lovely red hide!'